Chapter One

A RED-TAILED HAWK SOARED ACROSS THE HOT TEXAS SKY looking down at the ground with keen, golden eyes. It was, as always, looking for food. Rabbits were best—fat and passive once caught, a careless hare would keep the bird of prey sated for a couple of days. But anything would do; a rodent, a snake, even a tarantula would keep hunger at bay. Unfortunately, pickings were slim today and the hawk let out a piercing cry of frustration.

Then, it veered sharply to the right as it spied a great, brown wall of dust rising from the ground more than a hundred feet into the air. These giant uplifts of loose dust, gravel and dirt were common lately as drought had settled onto the land more than a year earlier. The bird hissed and rode a thermal around the dust storm to begin its search again but braked in midair with a startled squawk as the front wall of the storm disgorged a horse and its rider.

Both man and animal were completely covered in dust, but the horse picked its way surefootedly through the scrub brush and cactus in its path and the man pulled a kerchief off his lower face and blinked dirt from his eyes. A thin trail led down into a valley and the man urged his horse down the deer path. He gazed up at a red-tailed hawk as it whistled, flapped its wings and sailed off out of sight.

Jack Ballard rode his buckskin down through the rocks and sagebrush. He sat his horse with confidence but no urgency. The blazing Texas sun had both horse and rider sweat-soaked; yet unbending, they moved to the bottom of the ravine and headed across the dusty, parched prairie land which shimmered with the heat of the day.

Jack brought his horse to a stop and gazed at the grass-starved valley. His cool hazel eyes took in a thicket of mesquite in the near distance, and further on a range of blue-green mountains. As he studied the far horizon, he spied two riders, moving diagonally toward him. He frowned momentarily, then clicked his tongue and continued.

He was a man in his early thirties, and handsome in his own way. Not conventionally so; his over-long whiskers shadowed a sun-toughened face and his once straight nose was slightly crooked… a testament to his fair-share of frontier justice. At 5' 11" and 200 pounds, he sat his handsome horse with the grace of a much smaller man.

He was in a fancy, low-horned, double-cinched saddle, and dressed neither plainly, nor in arrogance save for the .44-40 Colt on his hip. High in its holster, two inches of a seven-inch barrel gleamed from the end of the holster. A Winchester carbine was slung in a scabbard up by the

NO MAN'S LAND

A Jack Ballard Novel

LINELL JEPPSEN
JEB ROSEBROOK

WOLFPACK
PUBLISHING
— EST 2013 —

No Man's Land
a jack ballard novel

Linell Jeppsen
Jeb Rosebrook

Paperback Edition
Copyright © 2018 Linell Jeppsen, Jeb Rosebrook

Published in the United States by Wolfpack Publishing, Las Vegas.

Wolfpack Publishing
6032 Wheat Penny Avenue
Las Vegas, NV 89122

wolfpackpublishing.com

Paperback ISBN 978-1-64119-154-8

Cover art: Charles M. Russell "Roundup #2," oil on canvas, 1913, Public Domain

NO MAN'S LAND

swells and a canteen hung off the saddle horn along with a coiled 40-foot rope.

An hour or so later, Jack saw the outline of a ranch in the near distance and came up on a hand-written sign which read:

SWAIN CATTLE COMPANY
BIG RIVER, TEXAS

Hearing hammering coming from the ranch, Jack approached through the bottomland of river where now only dust-covered corn and potatoes remained beside a grass-thin pasture which was home to a pair of horses and a slat-ribbed Guernsey milk cow. He looked ahead to the ranch. A windmill rose above a grove of cottonwoods, an adobe house, a barn and a corral.

Dogs barked madly as they raced out to meet him; four mongrels, one of which was followed by a batch of pups. The hammering stopped, and a middle-aged woman stepped out of the barn to see who had arrived. She was a strong, robust woman in her late forties with faded blonde hair, and sharp blue eyes.

She wore a wide-brimmed hat, and a faded blue shirt, buttoned to the collar. Her britches were stuffed into high-topped boots and held up by wide suspenders. Her face was red with the sun and heat, but pleasant enough as she took her measure of Jack Ballard. Gazing past him, however, her mouth turned down at the corners as she spied the other riders.

She glared at them and then turned toward Jack as he said, "Afternoon."

The riders were riding hard through a great tangle of

mesquite, cat-claw and palo verde trees to Kate's right. As the dogs began to growl, Jack dismounted and tipped his chin toward the approaching riders. "They belong to you?"

Kate ignored him and turned her attention toward the riders. "Cale! Troy... that's far enough!"

The two young men stopped their horses and stared as Jack started to take off his sweat-soaked shirt.

Cale Bolt was twenty and his brother, Troy, was seventeen. They gazed at Jack and then at each other. Ballard now had his shirt off and they both saw the big gun at his hip.

Kate, hollering now, continued, "Go on! Back where you come from!"

Cale grinned. "Why, we only come to watch you, Kate."

Troy looked to Jack, who was wringing the sweat out of his shirt and added, "Yeah, like him there!"

Kate frowned and looked toward Jack. "Well, you had your look, so go on and get!"

The young men stayed put, though, and Jack drew the Colt and tossed it to Kate. "Help yourself…"

She looked the gun over—dark wood butt, gold-inlay just above and below the trigger guard and filed-down hammer. She tossed it back and muttered, "No, thanks."

Looking at the Bolt boys, Ballard holstered the gun, and Cale smirked, "That was smart of you, Kate. There's two of us, after all, and we could always start shootin' back!"

Ballard smiled. "Might make things interesting, alright."

It was only a soft-spoken statement, nothing glib, but

there was something in it that caused the boys to start a little and look to each other.

Ballard's gaze didn't waver, and his hand dropped to rest by his gun. Kate stepped back a pace and the boys turned their horses slowly around. Their hands were on their guns but hesitant. Then, they abruptly spurred their horses and tore back through the thicket from which they came.

Ballard watched them go, a slight smile on his face. Then he turned to Kate. "My name's Ballard, Jack Ballard. Is Charlie Swain around?"

He watched a pulse of emotion cross Kate's face. A moment later, she shook her head, and said, "No."

ABOUT A QUARTER OF A MILE AWAY, Cale and Troy pulled their horses to a stop on a ridge. Looking back toward the ranch, Cale said, "I don't know who he is, but we'll deal with him just the same."

Then the brothers moved on in a gallop, leaving dust hanging in the air behind them.

Chapter Two

KATE, GLARING, WATCHED THE BOYS RIDE OFF AND THEN turned to Jack. "How long since you've had a bath and a change of clothes?"

Jack grinned. "That bad, huh?"

In no mood for jokes, she rolled her eyes and said, "Lead your horse behind the house to the water trough. I'll bring out some soap and a washcloth. Also," she looked him up and down. "I have some clothes I'm sure will fit you." Turning to walk inside, she added, "Don't get any soap in the trough."

Jack led his sweated buckskin around back toward the windmill, and the round water trough. He peeled his socks and pants off while his horse sucked huge draughts of water. He was standing there, near naked when Kate stepped out the back door with a bowl of warm water, soap and a washcloth. She had a shirt, socks and a pair of britches under her left arm.

She put the items on a log bench and turned back to

her house with the words, "I'm cooking up some dinner now. Come inside when you're cleaned up."

Jack scrubbed his skin raw, sighing with relief. It'd been at least three days since he'd jumped in a creek to rinse off, but he'd been forced to change back into clothes which were grimy with dust and sweat. He was surprised at how well the borrowed clothing fit. Assuming these were Charlie's duds, he resolved to take good care of them until his own clothes were washed.

Dressed, he glanced up and saw that dusk had fallen. The mongrel hounds were lazing under the cottonwood trees, and a few Dominique chickens pecked for bugs in the dust and weeds, ignored by the dogs. Jack studied the adobe house and saw that it was run-down with many antlers decorating the walls. Strings of green and red peppers were hung to dry, casting long shadows onto the porch.

Smoke from the chimney hung in the air and lifted lazy tendrils through the windmill's blades, which were not moving. He heard Kate's voice and turned toward the back door. She was turned sideways and pointing at something inside the house. "When you come inside my house, the gun goes right there."

Jack walked up and stepped inside. He saw a couple of pegs on the wall and hung his gun on one of them. He watched Kate move back toward a large black cook stove and turned to gaze at a portrait of a stern-faced, cold-eyed man. An 1860 model Colt hung on a peg on the other side of the photograph.

Kate put food and whiskey on the table behind him, and Jack asked, "How long you been widowed?"

There is a momentary silence, then she said, "One

hundred and thirty days." She sighed, adding, "He used to hang his gun on that peg. The other one's mine. Sit down."

Ballard sat at the table and placed a crumpled, dirty letter between them.

Kate looked at the envelope and said, "Help yourself, while I read your letter."

But he needed no invitation to the food. He was hungry and began working on the Frijoles, oven-bread and whiskey. He set to with such gusto, Kate paused to behold his appetite.

He grinned at her and exclaimed, "Ain't that fine handwriting? Only man I ever knew—Uncle Bob was—who kept him a special girl just to do his hand writing for him."

Kate nodded. "Charlie always did say your uncle was a 'Badlands' Ballard". She studied the letter for a moment and said, "Here, where he talks about horses…" She read out loud in a halting manner; "And, if you are still chasing the wild horses, Jack would be a good helper to you and yours, being expert on horseback and keen of mind and eye and hardly does he lack for courage…"

Considering the last line, Kate stared at Jack as he piled frijoles on the bread. She looked back to the letter and read, 'Signed, Robert Andrew Ballard, Abilene, Texas, dated this Independence Day, eighteen and seventy-five…'" Looking up, she exclaimed, "Why, this letter is three years old!"

With a shrug, Ballard reached for more frijoles, "Yup, I been keeping pretty busy." Then he gazed at her with no trace of humor, no fooling around.

Kate thought for a spell and cleared her throat. "A man could figure a horse trail—if someone was to show him where it was. But he would also find the fastest way to the far side of the border… that ain't your problem, is it?"

Jack sat still and silent, eating his dinner. A Grandfather clock in the corner of the room, with a glass panel on the bottom painted with the image of the capitol building in Austin, chimed the half-hour.

Ballard said, "There's a big demand up north for driving horses. Saddle ponies, too."

Kate nodded in agreement. "There's a real scarcity of law in these parts… you might know that. Or, it could be a coincidence that you don't."

He studied the woman and said, "Know where I can find wild horses, do you?" He added, "You'd be saving me some time and earning yourself some money by taking me to them…"

Kate said, "No treasure in this country is a secret to me. Not on your life, Jack." She paused a beat, "Of course, horses is as scarce as buffalo around here these days. But, up in the mountains—if you know where to look…"

Ballard murmured, "Horse buyers up in Omaha? Paying ten dollars a head."

She replied, "So, how bad do you want horses?"

"How many are there?"

Kate poured a drink and gulped it down in one throw. "It'd take the two of us to handle any such roundup. You know that, don't you?"

"I didn't hear an answer to my question…"

Kate looked at the far wall for a moment and answered, "I'd say… in the hundreds—two hundred, maybe. Used to be in the thousands."

Ballard pondered a moment and said, "If you're willing to prove that, we'll make ourselves a deal."

Kate shook her head. "If you don't mind, Jack, I'll be taking first shuffle on this hand…"

Ballard frowned. "Hold on, Kate! No horse trading before I see the horses!"

Kate stared at him a second and said, "Give me a week of your time. Working for me."

Ballard frowned. "Well, ranch chores ain't exactly my line of work…"

The woman shook her head. "Look, I need help. Riding fence—tending my cattle… what's left of them. I can't pay nothing, and the food's neither regular nor dependable."

Jack looked around. There was a Hawken Plain rifle above the hearth and the ever-present picture of Charlie Swain staring down at him. He glanced sideways at Kate and said, "No point in saying I'm not for sale, is there?"

Kate looked into his eyes and then sat up straight with a bright smile. "Wait a minute. I have an idea… why sure I do! I'll give you the first hundred head of horses we find. Yours—free and clear. At ten dollars a head, that's a thousand dollars in your jeans!"

Ballard said, "Now, just slow down there, Kate. You say you're going to trade over to me a thousand dollars' worth of horses for a week's worth of work?"

Kate poured herself another slug of whiskey and shrugged. "Could be two weeks. You never know."

Ballard sat back in his chair. "Figuring there are horses to be found, kind of makes you pretty desperate, don't it?"

Her eyes flared with anger. "Desperate! A year without a drop of rain? That's enough to make anyone desperate!"

Ballard nodded, and stood up. He walked over to where his gun was hanging on the peg.

Kate, pleading now, said, "You're a busy man. I can see that. I ain't so selfish to not pay for the time and work I could use from you…"

Ballard studied Charlie Swain's photograph again and asked, "He die natural or otherwise?"

Taking another swig, Kate answered, "Oh, it was what you might call a natural affliction of the heat. Otherwise mended by a bullet…"

Jack saw moisture glistening in Kate's eyes and then she snapped, "It can happen, you know. Especially when you take a mind to kill yourself." She stared at Jack hard, adding, "I buried his gun with him."

Jack sighed. "Just gave up, did he?" Then he waked back to the table for one more shot of whiskey.

Kate gazed up at him a moment and said, "Bunk's made up for you—in the bunkhouse. How long you plan to use it?"

Her question hung in the room and Jack downed his drink. "No more'n a week."

Chapter Three

_____

JACK MADE HIS WAY TO THE BUNKHOUSE CARRYING A borrowed lantern high to light his way. It was full dark now and a big, yellow moon heaved its way over the distant mountains. Stars were starting to pop as well, giving out enough light to illuminate his buckskin, standing hip-shot by the rail fence. Jack let out a soft, two-tone whistle in greeting and his horse nickered in reply.

He opened the door to the bunkhouse and saw that it was dusty but fairly-well in order. He spied a bunk with a thin pillow and two old horse blankets by the far wall. Fatigue was sneaking up on him. His eyes felt weighted down by the long miles on horseback, the crushing heat, the good food and warm whiskey.

He dropped his saddlebags by the bed, took his boots off and fell back on the pillow with a sigh. Within minutes, he was on horseback again in roiling clouds of dust, frantically chasing after the multi-colored rumps of his hundred wild horses. Panicked whinnies filled the air, and the thunder of hoofbeats sent Jack sailing into the deepest slumber he'd had since leaving Austin.

ABOUT FOURTEEN MILES AWAY, as the crow flies, another frantic chase was underway as Henry Chance laid a liberal whip across the hindquarters of his fancy chestnut horses. The horses squealed at this unusual harsh treatment and dug their hooves into the dusty trail at a full gallop. Chance, knowing that a celebration at this point was not only premature but foolish, couldn't help but let out a boozy bellow of triumph as his horses and wagon gained speed on their pursuers.

The celebration was brief, however, as the Bolt brothers almost immediately gained what ground they'd lost. Henry laid to with his whip again and yelled, "Come on, lads… you can do it!"

Never having lost grip on the whiskey bottle in his right hand, he took a deep pull, his long gray curls falling past his shoulders in messy splendor. Henry might be a dissolute drunk, but he still had his pride which showed in his flaming, red frock coat and trousers. His wagon was painted in the same crimson red but for the gilt lettering on the sides advertising his occupation:

Henry Chance
Dowser ~ Water Witch ~ Diviner
Since 1865

Realizing that his bottle was now empty, Henry threw it with all his might back at the riders, narrowly missing the lead man, U.S. Bolt.

The road bed was so dry, great heaping piles of dust rose like storm clouds in the moonlight, partially concealing the four Bolt Brothers who rode after the trespasser with enthusiasm. The lead rider was tall and heavyset and at twenty-four, the oldest of them. He pulled a pistol from his holster, enraged at the bottles near miss.

Unfortunately, he was nearly as drunk as his quarry but not half as practiced in the art of inebriation, so his aim landed on his twenty-two-year-old brother Garland, who was shaking out a loop. Realizing his brother had a good idea going on, he dropped his aim and hollered, "Hang it on him, Garland! Hang it on him!"

Henry, alarmed now and realizing the seriousness of the Bolt's intentions, pulled a .45 Colt "Shopkeeper" model, short-nosed pistol from his shoulder holster. Turning around on the bench seat, and drunkenly trying to focus his aim on U.S. and Garland, he was shocked to see two more riders emerge from the dust cloud on the other side of the wagon. It was the two youngest Bolt's: Cale and Troy.

Summoning up some spit, Henry shouted, "I'm threatening your lives, boys!"

Receiving only derisive laughter in reply, Henry closed one eye and was pleased to see two U.S.' merge into one and would've squeezed the trigger, but Garland's loop settled over his shoulders. Before he knew it, he was flying through the air. Garland's rope had jerked his body clean off the wagon, and he hit the ground hard, with a groan.

As Henry lay gasping in the dirt, U.S. raced after the wagon and the two run-away chestnuts. Seizing control of the horse's reins, he jumped onto the wagon seat and rode it back to where Henry and his brothers waited. Coming to a stop, U.S. started throwing Henry's possessions onto the ground.

Henry, still drunk and mad as a hornet hollered, "What's the meaning of this?"

At almost the same moment, Garland asked, "You find it, U.S.? You got it?"

Suddenly, a foot-locker sailed out the back end of the wagon and hit the ground with a great puff of dust

Henry shouted, "Hey, that's mine!" as the brothers gathered around whooping with excitement.

Again, Henry asked, pleading this time, "Come on, boys... what's the problem here?"

Troy answered, "Trespassing, for one."

Henry groaned and struggled to sit up. "Well, blast it, how else am I supposed to get to town and back?"

"That ain't our problem, it's yours. But you've got another problem on your hands..." U.S. gritted.

Henry, sarcasm ever at the ready, replied, "Oh, and what might that be?"

Cale, sensitive to ridicule at any time, snarled, "You work for Kate Swain! Boys, bring him over here!"

Suddenly the air was filled with the roar of gun fire as Henry's footlocker jumped in the dirt like a live thing and the padlock attaching top and bottom flew off into the weeds. Garland bent over and started tossing books, notebooks, underwear, and most of Henry's fancy, multi-colored suits out onto the ground.

U.S. growled in frustration. "Move out of my light, Garland. I can't see for my work!"

Garland shook his head, though, and said, "I can feel it with my hands, U.S.! Skinny, with two branches..."

Henry, in a bellowing rage by now, screamed, "Bandits! Outlaws! Thieves! Assaulting nature's own secrets in the very vault of science! Oooooh!"

Then he fell silent as U.S. held a velvet-covered bundle in the air. He saw U.S. peel the velvet away to reveal his most prized possession; a witch-hazel forked, dowsing rod which was polished to perfection and gleaming in the moonlight. He whispered, "Have you boy's no reverence for what's sacred to a man?' Then, forcefully, "Put it back where you found it!"

The brothers cackled with glee, though, and Cale smirked, "Better watch yerself, U.S. I think he's fixing to call the ocean up on us!"

More laughter filled the air, and Henry grumbled, "Only in the hope that none of you reptiles is amphibious!"

U.S. shrugged. "Well, I know for a fact this witch stick ain't calling up so much as a water-hole for Kate Swain. I can tell you that much!"

Henry, never having held the wisdom to know when to shut-up, hollered, "Well, I got my loyalties!"

U.S. frowned, and as sudden as a snake strike, thrust the dowsing rod into Henry's face—coming close to putting out his right eye. Then, with a sneer, and one hand on either end of the twin branches, he broke the rod like a wishbone.

Throwing the two pieces of wood on the ground in front of Henry, he snapped, "And, we got ours!"

Henry shook his head, and answered, "You tend to your own luck. And, don't think you can break my spirit like you done my rod!"

Totally enraged by Henry's unrepentant attitude, U.S.

reared back and growled, "No? Well then, why don't we just give a try at bleeding it out of you. Cale!"

Cale moved forward, taking up dally with the slack of his rope and dropped the loop over Henry's body. "Ready to go fer a ride, Water Witch?"

Henry, suddenly sober, said, "You're asking for big trouble taking up against me *and* Kate!"

U.S. answered, "Well, trouble's where you find it, I reckon, and you found yours!"

He turned to Cale and nodded. Excited by the sudden spectacle, young Troy hollered, "Burn him to blisters, Cale!"

Cale spurred his horse and screeched, "Yeeeee-hawwwww!"

Right before he took off on his sled ride, Henry shouted, "You haven't heard the last out of my name! None of you!"

Then he went head over heels. Cale was wasting no time. Henry took a rough and tumble over dirt, brush, cacti and rocks and his favorite red suit was ripped to shreds. His hat was tied on his head, but after a good knock or two, he came close to scraping away his vanity.

Finally, he managed to flip over onto his back, and commenced to staring up into the sky, where it seemed the very stars were keeping pace with him, all the way to unconsciousness.

———

About four hours later, the only sounds to be heard in and around the Swain ranch bunkhouse were the rickety whirring of a lone cricket's wings, and Jack's soft snores.

Then, a creak as the bunkhouse doors eased open to reveal the silhouette of a man's figure.

The response from the far side of the room was so sudden, so extreme, Henry could only stop and stare in shock at the Colt pistol which seemed to be aimed at a point right between his eyes.

He was torn and tattered, sporting two black eyes, and a bloody chin, but the lightning-quick pistol action caused him to draw up in wounded dignity. There was only a slight quaver in his voice as he declared, "You are sleeping in my bed!"

Then he sighed in weary resignation as the pistol-man shrugged and laid back down to resume his slumber.

Chapter Four

THE NEXT MORNING, JACK STEPPED OUT OF THE BUNKHOUSE and stared up at the sky. It was the color of old brass and promised to be another scorcher. Hearing a bell tinkling in the distance, he looked to his left and saw that Kate was already up and leading her milk cow from a pile of hay just outside the pasture fence toward where he stood.

A rooster crowed as she walked up and let the cow drink from the trough. She said, "I got some plans for your days' work…"

He nodded, but answered, "Kind of crowded. For me being the only man around here…" He gazed pointedly toward the bright red wagon parked haphazardly in front of the bunkhouse.

Kate followed his gaze and frowned. "Him? Just one of the drifting kind." She shrugged and walked over toward the trees to grab a stick. Walking back, stick in hand she said, "Now, let me show you my property lines and where to find my cattle."

She drew a rough rectangle in the dirt at her feet, then

pointed to the right. "You'll go due west from here and after about a mile you'll run into the dividing fence line between my land and the Bolt's…" She sighed, and the corners of her mouth turned down again. To Jack's mind, she seemed desperately sad.

"I need you to head over to that hay rick with the wagon," she turned around to point at a small pile of hay, "and fill it with as much hay as you can. Also, take a couple of those buckets…" she pointed at two large wooden buckets by the trough, "and give the weaker ones some water. Most of the streams are dried up by now."

Jack nodded and walked over to the wagon where a horse was already hitched up and mouthing the tips of a sagebrush. Once seated on the bench he heard a thump from the back of the wagon. Looking around he saw that Kate had placed a wooden tool box inside. She gazed up at him and said, "Wire cutters, nails, and some wire in here, in case you see some fencing down."

He turned forward, slapped the reins and clicked his teeth. The wagon moved forward, and he drove around to the stack of hay. Frowning at the measly supply, he jumped down and forked the feed into the back of the wagon, then turned it around and picked up the two buckets Kate had already filled with water.

Ready to go and play ranch hand, he snapped the reins again and drove by the bunkhouse where Henry stood by the door. The older man was dabbing a washcloth at a long scrape on his chin, and glared at Jack as he moved past.

Jack shrugged and yelled, "Hee-aw!" at the lazy horse that was headed straight for another juicy sagebrush. The horse twitched a bit, and then headed west at a trot.

He'd driven about twenty minutes when he spotted a bunch of Longhorns in the distance. They were all thin and drought-hungry, their glossy red, black and brown pelts gray with dust. They were gathered around a cluster of mesquite and Smoke trees and had eaten all the leaves off the brush, reducing the grove into a skeleton forest.

The sight of these cattle; their plight, their magnificence reduced to such hunger, made Jack's chest tighten with pity. Unaccustomed to this kind of emotion however... and not welcoming it, he frowned and went back to the task at hand.

He crawled into the wagon and started forking hay to the now excited and bellowing cattle. It was good to see them dig into the hay, but he knew they would be unable to continue like this much longer.

Even as he thought about it, he looked up and saw a band of buzzards roosting in the upper branches of the Smoke trees. Glaring, he poured a half bucket of water into the bone-dry trough, then climbed aboard again and moved on.

Another 500 feet, or so, he heard a thin bleat and pulled the wagon to a stop. He could see the tip of a horn waving about by a patch of cactus. Walking up, Jack saw a brood cow lying in the dirt. She was unable to stand any longer and was dying. It was clear that she'd chewed up as much of the cactus as she could, and he saw that her mouth and tongue were thick with needles.

Gazing around, Jack saw another form lying close-by; a calf, maybe a week-old, trying to get milk from its mother. He brought water over to the brood and watched as she tried to drink, but was too weak. "Come on, gal" he murmured. "You got to try..."

He tried to pick the cactus spines from her tongue, but she swung her huge horns at him, as the calf bawled. Knowing he was doing no good at the front end, he walked around back and tried to lift her up by the tail, but she just groaned in agony.

Giving up on the brood, he bent down and picked the calf up in his arms. He saw the cow's eyes follow him as he took her calf away, but he placed it in the back of the wagon and put his canteen to the baby's mouth. The tiny animal gulped the liquid greedily, as Jack pulled his Colt, took aim and put the brood out of its misery.

JACK FOLLOWED the fence line for about three miles and saw a man repairing a portion of the fence with new wire. He looked up at Jack's approach, stood straight, tipped his hat back and said, "Howdy."

Jack nodded and stared past the man toward large piles of hay and sparkling, clean water filling several troughs to the brim. About forty cattle milled around eating hay and drinking the water. They were mostly fat, sleek and healthy. Hearing the calf in back of the wagon bleat again, he sighed in frustration.

The man spoke, "Name's Bolt. Jesse Bolt's oldest, Ulysses. U.S., I'm called. Reckon you be Kate's new man. The one who met my brothers yesterday."

Ignoring U.S.'s introduction, Jack said, "You must have a pretty good water supply."

U.S. glanced past him, taking in the rickety wagon, the small amount of hay and the starving calf. He spat and said, "We buy ours. Reckon my Pa'd give up his own life before he'd allow *his* cattle to die of hunger and thirst."

Jack asked, "How much would it cost to share his feed and water with Kate's cattle?"

U.S. frowned. "Charity ain't our business. Now, what's yours?" He bent to the fence and snipped off a piece of dangling wire.

Jack, seeing the hate in U.S.'s expression said, "I wouldn't go to the trouble of finding out…"

U.S. grinned and glanced at the fence. "You know, I sure hate repairing fences. I suspect it would be a whole lot easier to just tear one down… like this one."

He moved off toward his horse with an easy swagger, and Jack saw another group of riders approaching, driving cattle ahead of them toward the feed and water. *The other brothers*, he figured.

U.S. reached his horse and stepped up into the saddle. Just as he gained his seat, Jack said, loud enough for U.S. to hear; "Depends on which side of the fence you're on."

With those words, he slapped the reins and headed out, as U.S. watched him go, eyes narrowed in anger.

A few hours later, finished with his work and now heading towards the ranch, Jack came across a grave and a marker that stated;

CHARLES SWAIN
1828-1878
He Owned Land

Jack stepped off the wagon and looking past the gravesite saw two tall fence posts. One had the Bolt brand hanging from it, the other announced the Swain brand.

He looked down and saw a seething mound of gray and brown feathers moving over another dead steer. He threw a rock at the buzzards, but they paid him no mind and continued to pick the carcass clean.

Jack moved around to the back of the wagon, and stopped when he saw that the calf had died. He shook his head and started to carry the animal over toward the industrious scavengers. He had no sooner set it down on the ground, when a shot rang out. He dropped flat and heard a bullet plow into a fencepost, fifteen yards away.

He grabbed his pistol from its holster and waited, hearing only the wind picking its way over the dry plain, and the distant lowing of Bolt's cattle. Finally, sensing that the threat had passed, he climbed back onto the wagon bench, clicked his teeth and set off toward his temporary home.

Chapter Five

ABOUT A HALF MILE AWAY FROM THE RANCH, JACK SCREWED his lips up in disgust. His whole body was covered in dust —from his boots to his ears. There was even dust in his mouth! He could feel it grinding between his molars. He unscrewed the cap on his canteen, took a swig, swished the liquid around in his mouth and spat a brown puddle onto the ground.

Then he took another pull off the canteen, swallowed and stared into the wickedly bright sun which was sizzling on the horizon above the ridge line in the distance. He recalled, suddenly, why he had given up, so long ago, on ranching to begin with. All those long days covered in dirt and sweat, always a slave to nature's whims, forever only one season away from catastrophe... no thanks.

He couldn't wait to move on from this failing farm; find his wild horses, sell them to the highest bidder... maybe find a soft pair of arms to hold him for a month or two. Jack saw a shadow in front of the adobe farmhouse. Blinking sunspots away from his eyes, he focused and saw a fancy black buggy, with its black parasol, hitched to a coal-black Morgan mare.

Jack drove the wagon around the front of the house to the trough in back. He un-hitched the gelding from the traces, and watched it drink. Then he pulled his hat off, dunked it in the trough and poured the water over his head and neck. He cupped his hands and splashed water over his face as well, and heard Kate holler from the back door, "Jack, put that hoss in the pasture and come in here when you're done. I need you."

He did as Kate instructed, and as he stepped up on the front porch he heard, "... and therefore, the power of attorney is hereby given by the party of the first part... the Lightning B Cattle Company, Jesse Bolt, owner, to said, Hiram Flint... which, of course, means the Bank of Brazos. My bank."

Jack pulled open the screen door and stepped inside. He saw a medium height, skinny man in a shiny black suit with a red carnation boutonniere. He was immediately reminded of a Black Widow spider. The man was holding a set of legal papers in his hands, and glaring down at Kate who was pouring herself a healthy slug of whiskey.

Henry Chance was sitting in the corner, glaring at Jack with dislike. He, too, had a half-full glass of whiskey in his hand.

Kate said, "You and your party of the first part... You're getting about as persistent as a case of the chiggers!" Then, looking up at Jack, she said, "Hiram Flint, meet Jack Ballard." She stared up at Flint with defiance, and added, "He works for me."

Pointing to a place next to where she sat on the couch, she said, "Sit down, Jack."

Jack sat while Hiram took in the pistol on his hip, and Henry Chance looked like a snarling bulldog chained in the corner of the room.

Kate looked at the two men and said, "I think you two have already met."

Jack nodded as Henry raised his glass in a mocking salute.

Anxious to drive his point home, Hiram picked up his papers again and waved them under Kate's nose. "Like I said," he continued. "Authorizing the Bank of Brazos to offer fifty cents per each of one thousand acres..."

Kate butted in, "Hiram here, has been trying to get me to sell for the last six months!" she was staring straight at Jack, asking him for some sort of impossible assistance.

Hiram, impatient with the interruptions, said, "If you don't mind..."

But Kate shot back, "But, I do mind! Why don't you plan on this being your last visit?"

Hiram took a deep breath and replied, "That's up to Jesse..."

"Well, why don't you tell him I have enough dogs raising their hind legs on my property without you adding to them!" Then she gave a wicked smile. "Or, are you and your bank hiding behind Jesse... using him?"

Hiram said, "Well, Kate, right now it's good business for him to buy and for you to sell." He glanced over at Charlie's picture on the wall adding, "Before your loss becomes even greater than it's already been..."

Kate tossed back another drink and shook her head. "Well, fifty cents an acre is one loss too many for me!"

Hiram shot back. "Then, what about your daughter's education?"

Jack was shocked but masked his emotions well.

Kate, with a hard look at Hiram, poured more whiskey into her glass as Hiram continued, "Look. You're nearly broke. Wouldn't you like to have enough money to be sure Jewel finishes her schooling?"

For the first time since entering the house, Jack saw Kate's hard-case exterior crack—just a little, but she surprised him by saying, "I ain't selling, dammit! And Jesse don't get to cut my fences and run me off, neither!"

Hiram growled, "Who cut her own fence first, huh? You did. Trying to steal Jesse's water and feed for your own cattle!"

Jack looked at Kate and saw that Hiram's words were true but again, Kate surprised him by saying, "Among neighbors, survival is everyone's business! If one man can pay to haul water and feed, then he can damn well share with the rest of us."

Hiram, staring at Jack sneered. "And, just to make sure of that, you brought *him* here… a hired gun!"

Hiram challenged Jack with his eyes, but Jack only stared straight ahead, neither affirming or denying the charge.

Kate stood up and shouted. "He's no such thing!" She appeared to be well into her cups by now.

But Hiram just looked away from Jack and said, "I suppose you're going to tell me he didn't threaten those two, young Bolt boys yesterday?"

Kate shook her head. "I don't care what they told Jesse, but I *will* give you something to tell him…" She slugged down her whiskey and said, "You can pass along the news to Jesse that I got me a professional, all right." She smiled sweetly at a very cautious Jack. "You tell him I hired me a professional well-driller. You bet! Come clear from Nebraska!"

She grinned at the shock on Hiram's face. "Rare combination, too… strong mind and strong hands. He's getting Nebraska wages, too. A dollar a foot!"

Hiram was staring at Jack with deep suspicion, but Kate reached over to the banker and tugged at his shiny, black sleeve with the greatest confidence. Un-heard by Kate, Henry leaned his straight-backed chair against the wall, looked up at the ceiling and whispered, "Oh, oh… here we go again…"

Kate continued, walking back a few steps to sit close to Jack on the couch. It was all he could do to keep from scooting away. "Only, Hiram… well-drilling ain't what brought Jack here. Nossir! He's here on family business!"

She grabbed Jack's arm, and gazing happily up at him, she said, "He's here to marry my Jewel… my precious daughter, Jewel!"

Flint looked sharply at Jack who managed a weak smile, as Kate nuzzled his cheek with boozy affection. Chance closed his eyes.

"Quite a handsome pair to mingle bloods, wouldn't you say, Hiram? My Jewel and this Jack?"

Hiram grudgingly agreed, "Quite."

Smiling, Kate said, "Matter of fact… Jack here is off to Noble Hall tomorrow, to fetch Jewel back home!"

Jack wanted to clap his hat on his head and run out the door.

But Kate was relentless. She continued, "To make plans for the wedding, and all." Turning to gaze up at Jack, she said, "Jack—tell Hiram how happy you are! Speak for yerself, lad."

Hiram's gaze swiveled to Jack who just managed to choke out, "You could say, I got no words to say what's on my mind."

Henry grinned in enjoyment of Jack's discomfort, no stranger apparently, to Kate's machinations.

Jack stood up, and said, "Now, if you'll excuse me, there's a lot of work between me and tomorrow."

Turning around to head out the door, he gave Kate a loaded look, and was gratified to see her wilt a bit.

To his back, Hiram said, "You certainly wasted little time establishing yourself."

To which Jack answered, "Hard to keep up with, ain't it?" he looked to Kate again and then stepped outside, slamming the front door behind him.

Hiram stood undecided, for a moment, and then picked his contract up once more and shook the papers. "Lies!" he hissed. "This is a scheme… a dollar a foot… marrying your daughter! I think it's time to take my leave."

Kate smiled. "At least I can give you credit for knowing when to leave!"

Hiram mocked her sarcastic smile, then turned abruptly, put his black bowler hat on and stormed out the door, slamming it even harder than Jack had upon leaving.

Kate sat back down on the couch with a sigh of relief and poured one more drought of liquid courage as Henry

Chance applauded the moment by clapping his hands. One angry glance his way, however, stopped his antics and Kate bit her lip and stared at the twice slammed front door with fear.

Chapter Six

Jack stormed off the porch and marched toward the bunkhouse to fetch his gear and move on. Just like ranching—he'd had experience with lying women before and wanted no part of it now. No thanks!

He took his hat off and swatted it against his upper thigh in frustration. *Getting married to some mysterious daughter?* "Ha! Not on your life!" he grumbled and then slowed to a stop as he took in the falling dusk. Looking around, he frowned. By the time he grabbed his gear, saddled his horse and took off down the trail it would be full dark.

He was an experienced horse man and knew that risk to horse and rider increased by half when setting out in the dark on unfamiliar ground. Sighing, he decided to just go to the bunkhouse, get some shut-eye and leave at first light. He would go look for that horseflesh by himself.

He heard a door slam and turned around to see Flint exit the front of the house in a high snit. Jack saw the spidery little man jump into his fancy buggy, lay a hard whip on his fancy mare, and take off in a hurry.

Hiram yelled "Hiah!" and glared at Jack as he passed by. Jack matched the banker glare for glare and grinned when he saw all four of the ranch dogs chase after the buggy, growling and snapping. "Good riddance to bad rubbish", he murmured and started walking toward the bunkhouse.

He stopped, however, as Kate stepped out her door and walked toward him with her hands in her pants pockets. Her shoulders were hunched up around her ears as if anticipating a blow. Getting closer to him, she took her hands out of her pockets and raised them defensively. "I know what you're going to say..."

Jack frowned. Not much of an apology. "I've been lied to one too many times, Kate. I was shot at too." He turned around to proceed to the bunkhouse.

To his back, she hollered, "I know... I admit I was lying!"

He shrugged in disgust. "I'll go find my own horses!"

Kate stopped, stunned. "Jack, I just apologized! What more do you want?"

He stopped and turned around to look her up and down. "You might say you're sorry that one of your neighbors took a pot-shot at me!" It was obvious to him, she was as drunk as a lord, but he also saw that she was trying to gain some composure... and maybe a degree of her honesty.

She lifted her hands in an airy shrug, and mumbled, "All right! I'm sorry 'bout that, but I'm not surprised. You saw how those boys are!"

Jack shook his head. "This place is more trouble than it's worth."

Kate said, "Jack, listen to me. I'm nearly broke. I admit it. But I won't pay for my girl's education by selling out my land!" Angry tears sparkled in the dusk.

She continued. "Which means Jewel will have to come home. Nothing permanent, mind you. Just until the prospects improve. This land will pay its way, again. Always has."

Still angry, Jack shrugged and started walking again—Kate hot on his heels. He looked around at the shabby house, the parched land, the dry creeks and thought, *Prospects? What prospects? Sure, maybe this land will produce again, but right now it's on the verge of collapse, holding on through nothing but the sheer will of a stubborn lady.*

"Jack!" Kate plucked at his shirt. "Jack, please! I need someone to go fetch my girl home."

Jack tipped his chin toward Henry's red wagon. "Have him do it."

"No!" she cried. "I ain't about to let my daughter think there's anything between me and that… that water witch!"

Jack stopped walking and stared at her. "Then *you* go!"

Suddenly, a tear swelled up and started running down her cheek. She bowed her head, and kicked the toe of her boot around in the dirt. "I… I ain't been near a town in fifteen years… much less inside the walls of that fancy school. Charlie—he always carried her back and forth," she paused a moment and Jack could have sworn she was blushing.

She added, "I mean… all you have to do is look at me to know I ain't got the faintest fragrance of a lady about me!"

For a moment, Jack was moved but he brushed sentiment aside and took a few more steps toward the bunkhouse, Kate right beside him. She said, "You know… I don't even own a dress."

Jack stopped and stared. Again, she had disarmed him with her honesty. She smiled up at him, and admitted, "I borrowed one once, though!"

He shook his head at her girlish grin, but she added, "It was made out of silk. Silk!'

He watched as she clutched her calloused hands together as if in remembrance of a long ago, never forgotten bouquet. "Silk it was… borrowed from a fine lady. Mind you—the wife of an officer in the United States Tenth Cavalry!"

She smiled and for just a second, Jack saw the young lady she'd once been. Long yellow hair, wide blue eyes, a sweet, pointed chin.

"Oh, we was matching hour-glass figures in those days —in the spring of twenty-six years ago." She smiled dreamily. "Bound up the Missouri we was, on the Mary Beth. And the captain of that good ship spoke marriage vows between me and a hard case of love named Charlie Swain."

She frowned. "But, that was the last time I cared about wearing a dress, don't you know? Because from then until his death me and Charlie was partners to this land, Jack. Faithful to the mountains and desert, alike. In any season."

She gazed up at him and said, "Please. Bring my girl home."

Jack looked down at his own boots, and sighed. Then he nodded and said, "All right. But then I'll be movin on."

Looking more hurt by this than triumphant over her

victory, Kate said, "Thank you, Jack." And then, "Well, I'd better get supper on the table."

She turned and hurried away, as Jack stared after her, thinking, "How she does convince."

Then he headed to the bunkhouse to get some rest.

Chapter Seven

As Jack lay dozing in the bunkhouse, Henry poured another generous shot of whiskey into his and Kate's glasses. It wasn't that often he had a chance to be with Kate alone, and he planned to take advantage of the opportunity.

He had been in love with Kate Swain from the first time he'd clapped eyes on her, even while she still had a husband. She was strong, disciplined and willing to go to great lengths to acquire what she wanted in life; pretty much his polar-opposite which Henry thought was a fine thing. He knew that love, as in nature, should be an equal measure of Yin *and* Yang to prevail.

Henry could tell she'd been a beauty in her younger days, as well. Even now she was a handsome woman for her age. Being no spring chicken himself, he felt that they would suit well as a couple. If only he could convince her of that fact…

Her voice rang out behind his back. "You know, Charlie made sure there was a good stock of whiskey to see us through, but I reckon he didn't plan on some drifter drinking all my stores after he was gone."

Henry froze in mid-pour. Turning around, he replied, "Kate, I was just pouring you a drink. Been a hard day for you, I know." He smiled his most winsome, and held her glass out in offering.

She rolled her eyes, and said, "I ain't feeble, Henry. I can pour my own drinks. Now, why don't you head out to your bed? I'm weary to the bone."

Henry said, "You know I would, Kate, but that… gunslinger took my cot and all the coverings!"

Kate frowned. She hadn't given the sleeping arrangements in the bunkhouse the slightest consideration, and realized now that she had, indeed, given Henry's bed to Jack. She shrugged and said, "Forgot about that. Follow me, and I'll fetch you a pillow and a couple of blankets."

Kate turned around and started walking toward the back of the house, and Henry swallowed his whiskey while her back was turned. Then he walked after her and received two old blankets and a thin tick pillow to make up a cot in the bunkhouse.

Still put-out that that young scamp had commandeered his bed, Henry tried once more. "You know, Kate. What with the Bolts and now Flint troubling your doorstep, maybe I should stay in here… for your protection and all."

Kate shook her head. "Not on your life, Mister. You either stay out there or go on your way. Makes no nevermind to me."

Henry sighed. "Okay, Kate. Whatever you say."

She marched to the back door, swung it open and said, "I trust you're still witchin' for water around here?"

Henry, stepping onto the back porch, paused and said, "Of course I am. You'll see me dousing to the east come tomorrow, I promise."

Kate nodded, and replied, "I'll be checking, too. Good night."

Then the door shut firmly in Henry's face.

———

ABOUT SIX MILES AWAY, a heated discussion was taking place in the Bolt mansion. Hiram's buggy was parked in front of the once elegant but now tarnished and run-down, two-story, plantation-style mansion which thrust up out of the Texas plains like a sore thumb.

Jesse Bolt's wife, Sarah, had come with a pretty penny when he'd married her, and one of her demands when being hauled out to the stark (and in her mind, ugly) Texas prairie was to have a beautiful house just like the one she'd grown up in and was now forced to leave.

Jesse didn't mind, although he sometimes felt a twinge of embarrassment at his overly opulent home. Still, after Sarah was carried off by childbed fever, and Jesse was left to raise his four sons alone, the house had fallen into disrepair.

JESSE BOLT'S sons lounged about on the front porch, drinking whiskey and finishing off their chicken dinner as Hiram ranted and raved inside the house.

As the boys eavesdropped on Jesse and Hiram, chickens and goats wandered about the once resplendent rose gardens which were now filled with thorny leafless shrubs, farm implements, discarded tools, and a month's worth of rubbish.

U.S. frowned as he heard Flint shout, "She's not selling! Neither are the others."

Jesse replied, "Corn whiskey and bluff. That's all she's made of."

Hiram answered, "I don't think she's bluffing, Jesse. As long as she stays, the others will too! Now, what are you going to do about it?"

The boys heard a chair scrape across the floor boards and heard their father say, "Well, since our salesmanship ain't worked, guess we'll just have to take a harder line."

Hiram growled, "I wish they would just come out here and fight you!"

Jesse answered, "Let's take a walk, Hiram…"

The boys sat back in their seats and tried not to let on they'd been listening as Jesse and Hiram stepped down off the porch stairs and made their way toward Jesse's watchtower.

———

FLINT STOOD on the platform of the watchtower, twenty-five feet in the air, as Jesse hunched over a telescope studying the horizon.

Jesse was a handsome man of forty-six, with cold, Ahab eyes. A strong man caught in the tough desperation of this drought, the binds of money promises and a dry land, getting drier.

Impatient, Flint said, "If you ask me, I think you're all crazy. You and Kate alike. Day after day of looking for signs… what good has it done you, Jesse?"

Jesse stood up in agitation. His thick neck was criss-crossed with the thatch-work of the years. As he stood there in his shirt-sleeves, towering over the skinny banker, he knew he had no answer. He stared up at the moon for a moment and then said, "Remember the panic of '73? And I thought the price of cow meat meant bad times. And you, Hiram; you nearly lost your bank!"

Flint snapped, "Old times are gone, Jesse. For good. I've got to stay on my side of the money these days."

Jesse turned around and glared. "Your side of the money! You're talking to the man who purchased this property twenty-five years ago that got you started in the business of money!"

He paused and shook his head. "My God! You'd think you was going broke on the thirty percent interest you got me paying you!"

Hiram drew himself up and barked, "When was the last time you made an interest payment? Eight months ago, that's when! But my bank's loan money is still keeping you in water and feed. . . "

Jesse answered, "And, why not? I gave you my word, didn't I?"

Hiram pulled papers from his pocket. "Your word wouldn't have meant a dime without collateral, Jesse! Which you have yet to deliver. Now, you were the one who told me those small timers across the river wouldn't last out the drought... that they'd pick up and move out..."

Jesse shook his head. "Using their land and bad times as my collateral was your idea!"

Flint waved the papers around again. "And you signed for it!"

Jesse grabbed the papers and threw them off the watchtower and down into the night.

Hiram glared and hissed, "You've got two weeks."

Jesse took a step back. His mouth dropped, and he stammered, "What do you mean, two weeks?"

Flint said, "I mean, I have committed the collateral you have failed to deliver as promised… ten thousand acres across the river."

Jesse snarled, "You mean you stole it?"

Flint shrugged. "Big land syndicate out of Denton. Seventy-five cents an acre! And I gave them my word and my signature to back it up." He studied Bolt's face for a second and added, "Now, you either deliver or my bank will take away your land and this ranch will be history."

Bolt's sons, standing under the watchtower turned to stare at one another in dismay. They heard their father say, "And to think… I put you in business on a handshake!"

Flint just shrugged. "The times, Jesse. Like business, they change."

Jesse, enraged, balled up his fist and growled, "Get out of my sight. Get out of my sight before I topple you from it!"

Hiram, nervous now, stepped onto the rungs of the ladder, but snapped, "Two weeks!" Then he headed down the steps to the ground below.

Jesse hollered after him, "There's no law for two hundred miles in any direction! Not you or no bank is fool enough to mess with me and mine!"

On the ground now, Flint stared up at Jesse and shouted, "If you and your boys can't handle Kate, let me know. I'll send you one who can!"

Jesse answered, "I'll be bound for Hell before I'd ask for your help!"

Flint shrugged and turned to leave but suddenly found himself surrounded by the Bolt brothers. He smiled, and said, "Why, evening boys."

Jesse threw down one last statement. "I can handle my own, Hiram!"

And U. S., angry and puffed up with swagger added, "And he's got us backing him."

Flint held his pleasant smile and wormed his way past the wall of young men, then walked briskly to his black buggy. Once inside, he cracked his whip and took off, hearing Jesse Bolt shout, "I am the eagle bird in this country, Hiram!" Then, "It was my money built your bank… ME!"

After watching Flint's buggy disappear into the darkness, Jesse looked down at his sons who were staring up at him from the ground.

"We'll handle this, boys. Just as sure as I say so…"

Chapter Eight

Jack left early the next morning. The house was dark, but he met Kate standing by the corral, holding the reins of a small mare, already saddled. "This is Jewel's horse… she named her Bonny."

Jack took the reins and nodded. Then Kate said, "The school is just past town-about three miles. Used to be a person could ride right through Jesse's land, but not now. Which means you'll have to skirt around his property line. Adds about eight miles to the trip."

Kate handed Jack a hand-drawn map and a gunny sack. "Lunch for you and my daughter. See you back here after dark." Then she turned on her heel and marched toward her house.

Jack shook his head at her stiff formality and mounted up. Turning the horses west, he headed toward the distant mountains and the *Noble Hall Academy for Young Ladies.*

The wind was fetching up a bit this morning and he could see storm clouds forming over the shadowed peaks. He wondered if this land's drought might be washed clean today, but dismissed that notion almost immediately. Although the foothills and mountains seemed to loom over him, he knew they were at least seventy miles away. If those clouds did bunch up and rain, they would probably be trapped by the very landscape which had formed them to begin with.

Looking ahead, he saw an archway to his left and a long, wide road leading off into the horizon. He also saw what looked like a watchtower. The sign hanging from the arch read;

BOLT LIGHTNING RANCH

A SMALLER, newer-looking sign nailed to the uprights read;

NO TRESSPASSING!
Violators will be shot!

JACK SHOOK HIS HEAD. Not very friendly; these Bolts. Then he kicked his horse up into a trot. By Kate's map, there was another twelve miles between here and Jewel Swain.

The wind picked up, plucking at Jack's clothes and teasing the horse's tails. The mare snorted nervously. She was a bit barn sour, he assumed, and didn't trust the winds tricky twists and turns.

Here and there, Jack saw dust devils rising out of the ground like gusty, spiraling spooks leading the way toward Jewel's school. Frowning, Jack knew that if he were prone to superstition, he might view natures frolics as a bad sign. Thankfully, he was not.

He drew near to town and halted his horse. Looking about, he spied a road leading around the town proper and on toward the west. He chose that path. He was not particularly worried about running into anyone who might wish him harm, but he also knew that trouble sometimes came calling when a man least expected it. He had no time for that this morning.

He pulled his watch from his vest and saw it was about eleven o' clock. It would be a long day and an even longer time fetching this girl back home. Looking up, he heard a bell tolling and saw a cluster of adobe building in the near distance.

The Noble Hall Academy for Young Ladies sat alone on the prairie and was surrounded by a pocket of trees bent with the sweep of wind and blowing dust. The buildings were modest, plain unpainted adobe and practical save for the fancy, black wrought-iron fence that surrounded it. It looked like there was one two-story dormitory building, a school house and a chapel. A flagpole rose up and quivered with the flapping of the U.S. and Texas flags it supported.

A sign on the heavy black gate said;

Noble Hall Academy for Young Ladies
Offering a Christian Education in the Refinements
of Needlework, Music and the Arts
Miss Corinne—Headmistress

Inside the chapel, Miss Corinne stood in the pulpit.

She was in her mid-forties, pale, thin and severe. Dust pummeled the window behind her as she cried out, "Good morning, young ladies!"

She was answered with, "Good morning, Miss Corinne!"

Miss Corinne announced, "This nooning, we will sing Hymn Four-Thirty-Two before our luncheon. We have a special treat for you today…" She smiled, and added, "We will sing this one standing up before heading into the dining hall!"

The girls, ages fourteen to twenty, in all sizes and shapes, stood as one with their hymn books in hand. They all wore conforming uniforms of gray Balmoral skirts and white Paletot jackets. Their dress code and total lack of make-up or jewelry reflected the spartan, Puritan environment evident in the chapel and surrounding buildings of Noble Hall.

Another girl sat across from the pulpit at a piano and at Miss Corinne's signal she set to with teenage exuberance.

———

JACK, approaching from the east, suddenly heard a chorus of feminine voices;

> *"Sowing in the morning*
> *Sowing seeds of kindness*
> *Sowing in the noon-tide,*
> *And the dewy eve…"*

Jack saw a middle-aged Indian woman, Kiowa maybe,

standing by the gate, watching his approach. She wore a keyring around her waist and was singing;

> *"Waiting for the harvest,*
> *And the time of reaping,*
> *We shall come rejoicing,*
> *Bringing in the sheaves..."*

Jack stepped down off his horse and tied the reins to a hitch-rail by the gate. He looked to the Indian woman and at the gate—waiting as she finished singing the song.

> *"Bringing in the sheaves,*
> *Bringing in the sheaves,*
> *We will come rejoicing,*
> *Bringing in the sheaves."*

FINALLY, SHE SAID, "YOU CHRISTIAN?"

Jack paused and studied the ground at his feet, considering. Then he said, "Sometimes…"

Unimpressed, the woman frowned and snapped, "No come here with gun!"

Jack gave her a look and unbuckled his gun belt as she watched carefully. He placed his gun and bullet-filled belt on a nearby rock, as the woman and girls inside began a new verse of "Bringing in the Sheaves."

Chapter Nine

Jack waited, impatiently, for the gatekeeper to finish her song. She stopped singing, finally, and removed her long black shawl. She then opened the gate a crack, placed the shawl cautiously over his gun and belt and let him onto the school grounds. Moving ahead of him up the steps, she said, "You wait here!"

She closed the door in his face and he waited as a swirl of dust buffeted him and Jewel's mare whinnied nervously. Finally, the door opened slightly, and the woman crooked her finger at him.

He stepped inside, smelled the yeasty odor of rising bread and heard a quiet murmur of feminine voices coming from the next room. A tall, thin, stern-looking woman was standing in the doorway. She placed her hands together and said, "My name is Miss Corinne. I am the headmistress here. How can I help you?"

Her voice was pleasant enough but her small brown eyes blazed with some inner fury. He smiled at her but received only a grimace of distaste in reply, so he plucked

Kate's letter from his pocket and handed it over. "This is from Kate Swain—Jewel's mother. She wants me to take Jewel back home for a spell."

She opened the letter and began reading as Jack watched her wipe his touch from her fingers on her long gray skirt, as if he carried the pox or was infested with a bad crop of fleas.

He frowned, thinking, *I wonder if the good folks around here know just how much this woman hates men?* Granted, many men gave cause for a woman's dislike, but all in all, most men cherished their wives, sisters, mothers and daughters. Why start these girls out on an emotionally hateful path in life? Other than to exact some sort of sly feminine vengeance on an unsuspecting, male species?

Jack glanced around at the school's interior. It was tidy, but dust had nevertheless wormed its long fingers through cracks in the walls, and had painted the wood floors with pale shadows.

Miss Corinne finished reading Kate's letter. She looked at him, and said. "Please, follow me. The girls are eating their supper now and won't appreciate the inter-ruption…" She started moving away and added, "We will serve you as well, but you'll eat in the kitchen."

Duly chastised, Jack followed the headmistress into a large dining hall. There were about fifteen long tables set in three rows, end to end. At the first sight of Jack, the hum of girlish conversation and the clink of silverware came to an abrupt halt. Stares, hard-held breath and sudden curiosity were directed at his tall, handsome cowboy gait as he followed Miss Corinne toward the front of the room.

It was, frankly, a novel experience for Jack as well, as

he stared about at the girls' faces trying to pick Jewel out of the crowd. Once or twice he met an inquisitive eye and a series of gasps and giggles swept across the room, causing the headmistress to take a ruler out of her skirt pocket and rap it sharply on a nearby table.

"Keep your eyes to yourselves, ladies!" she snapped. Immediately the girls bent over their porridge and bread. Then she announced, "Mister Jack Ballard for Miss Jewel Swain!"

There was an immediate buzz and twitter among the girls as Jewel lifted her eyes from her bowl and met Jack's gaze. She had been paying little attention to the man's entrance as she was particularly fascinated by the tiny piece of honeycomb adorning her plain porridge. It had been years since she'd tasted something so sweet. Still, as she met Jack's hazel eyes, her cheeks flushed. He was something just as sweet, to her eyes. And to think he was here for her!

Jack studied the young lady's face and saw that she did, indeed, resemble her mother. The same blue eyes, blonde-hair and pointed chin. But this girl was softer, sweeter than Kate and there seemed to be a shyness about her

Miss Corinne continued, "Your mother sent Mr. Ballard to fetch you home."

Jewel, ducked her head, not quite knowing what to do, and Miss Corinne snapped, "You may greet Mr. Ballard properly, Miss Swain."

Jewel rose to her feet and after a quick peek at Jack, held out her hand with a hint of a smile. "I am pleased to make your acquaintance, Mr. Ballard."

Jack nodded, and replied, "Call me Jack."

Jewel sat back down, and a fresh undercurrent of

twitter came from the girls, which was quickly stifled by a glare from the headmistress. Miss Corinne sniffed and said, "Come along, Mr. Ballard. We'll feed you in the kitchen."

Jack followed the stern lady but glancing at Jewel, he said, "As soon as you can pack…"

Jewel nodded. "I'll be prompt, I promise."

Jack moved away from her with a small grin.

She finished her cereal hastily, hardly even tasting the tiny piece of raw honey. She looked up for one last glance at the handsome man who had come to fetch her home and saw that he had also turned around and was gazing back at her. The girls at her table let out a giggle, and blushing, she finished her supper and fled up to her room to pack.

Chapter Ten

About a half hour later, Jewel ran down the steps of the schoolhouse with a battered satchel in her hand. She had changed out of her school clothes and now wore Texas buckskin leggings, her hat, and boots.

Jack couldn't help but notice how pretty she looked now that her hair had been sprung from its tight bun and flowed down the back of her chambray shirt in a long, golden braid. The girl smiled as she saw her mare, Bonny, and stood nose to nose with the horse; human and animal exchanging breath in a bond of friendship.

Jack tied her satchel on the back of his saddle and said, "If we keep up a good pace, we can arrive back home by supper time, maybe a little later."

Jewel looked at the large pistol he was strapping on, and answered, "Yes, let's do that. I want to."

They took off and rode side by side in silence until they passed the town and headed toward home. Jewel studied the clusters of tumbleweeds on either side of the road; a forest of unmoving flaxen refugees… witnesses to the hard drought they were in.

Jewel turned to the silent man riding beside her. "How long are you here for?" she asked.

Jack said, "Probably tomorrow. I'm getting me some of those wild horses."

Jewel drew back, and giggled slightly. "Horses… we haven't seen a wild horse in six years!"

One look at Jack's reaction, stilled her laughter. The man was frowning, and she realized immediately what had happened. Speaking softly, she said, "Ma does have that habit… saying what suits her one day and worrying about it the next."

Jack glared at her and then turned away in anger. Heart sinking, she said, "Maybe we should talk about something else. Should we?"

Jack spat, "How 'bout the weather?" Then he glanced sideways at her downcast eyes and was abruptly sorry. He knew there was no reason to blame Jewel for her mother's lies. He shrugged and said, "Sorry. I was counting on those horses."

Jewel nodded in reply.

The sun was boiling down on them, and Jack took his canteen from the saddle horn, unscrewed the lid, took a drink and offered the water to Kate's daughter.

Jewel took it with a small smile and after taking a drink, gave it back and turned toward him. "I remember the day rain finally came during the last drought. It was something. That was before my pa…" she gulped, and looked up at Jack's face.

He nodded in understanding and she continued, "Drought lasted for about six months that time, but when it finally did rain? Oh, what a gully washer it was! The three of us danced around like wild Indians, drinking the raindrops!"

She fell quiet again, and murmured, "Waiting for the rain can turn people crazy." Her blue eyes caught his and Jack realized that Jewel was pleading her mother's case.

He sighed, nodding in agreement. He knew, first-hand, what a drought could do to people, land, and animals. Desperation caught ahold of some folks, and greed over-took others. Some were swallowed by sorrow as they had to pack up and leave their dreams behind.

And, in Charlie Swain's case, utter despair; prompting him to check out early, leaving his wife and daughter to fend for themselves against the unforgiving elements, and predatory property owners like the Bolts.

He said, "Yeah, ain't nothing worse than nothing."

They came up on a fork in the road—one leading overland to Kate's ranch through the Bolt Lightning ranch, and the other circling around and causing eight more miles added to the trip home. Kate started to rein her mare to the left, through the Bolt's property.

Jack said, "Hold up there, Jewel."

She turned in her saddle and stared at him. "Why? It's a straight shot from here to home. The other way is much longer…"

Jack shook his head. "Sorry, but things have gotten pretty tense around here since you left for school. The Bolts are not taking kindly to trespassers these days."

"Trespassers…" she whispered. The girl looked doubtful but didn't argue. She turned her horse around and followed Jack down the much longer route toward home.

Neither one of them noticed the two young men watching their progress on a distant hillside.

Garland and Troy looked at each other, eyes opened wide with excitement. Then, without a word, they spurred their horses and galloped for home.

———

As THE TWO Bolt boys rode hellbent for leather toward home, Jesse Bolt sat in his living room staring at an old oil portrait of a handsome couple in 1850's dress clothes. He and his new bride, Sarah Cunningham. Wincing against the sweat dripping down his face, he scratched his head in confusion. He hardly even remembered the woman in the painting—and for the life of him, didn't recall her ever looking as hale and hearty as this rendering.

The dark hair and brown eyes were about right but not those rosy, red lips or the high-color on her cheeks. Jesse had often thought that Sarah was like a hot-house lily… healthy and beautiful under the most careful conditions but brittle and frail once exposed to real life.

She had begun to fade the minute she came to live with him in Texas, and each of her pregnancies had sucked what little of her vitality remained until, in the end, she'd wilted like a dead flower.

Jesse squirmed and rubbed at the crotch of his pants. He wanted a new woman… needed one. He was still a man in his prime, after all. He had considered asking the woman living next to him, but Kate was too prickly, too poisonous to even think of taking to wife. He suspected they would kill one another within weeks of their marriage vows.

He sniffed at an odor suddenly filling his nostrils. Glancing about, he saw that his once fine and expensive black walnut furniture was covered in dust, and his beautiful, long dining room table overflowed with dirty dishes, and left-over meals. Flies buzzed around his head, and he snarled in anger.

He was about to get up and shout at his boys to do some cleaning, when he sat back with a small sigh. The sound of raindrops hitting the metal roof filled his ears and soothed his temper. He wiped a handkerchief across his sweating face and allowed himself to relax and dream of better, greener times.

On the roof, U.S. and Cale were flinging pebbles and small rocks onto the tin to simulate the sound of rain. They had been at it for hours and both men were exhausted and drenched in sweat.

Cale called out, "U.S., my arms are about played out! When's Pa ever gonna say quit?"

U.S. gazed at his younger brother for a second, and replied, "When we get some real rain, I reckon."

Then, both of them turned and stared as Garland and Troy rode up whooping and hollering, "We seen them! We seen her... Jewel! We seen her!

Cale grinned, reached over and punched his brother lightly on the shoulder. "Oh-oh! Did you hear that? Jewel's back. Better get yourself all clean and shined up!"

U.S. licked his lips, eyes narrowed in speculation. He had wanted that girl for years, and a young man had his... needs.

Garland and Troy tore into the front yard still shouting, "Jewel! Coming home. Hired gun's with her!"

Jesse, hearing the boy's news, appeared in the front

door, a grin on his face. U.S. and Cale had climbed down off the roof and now stood facing their father. The mention of the "Hired Gun" brought a slight frown to Jesse's face.

But U.S. said, "Hey, Pa! What are we waitin' for? You want to catch up on a little business with Kate, don't you?"

Jesse studied the far horizon for a moment, then smiled. He thought, *Two birds with one stone... yessir. Get a beautiful young bride for my bed and maybe even a fine piece of property to go with her. That would keep that skunk of a banker, Hiram Flint, off my back!*

Turning to U.S., Jesse said, "You're right. I do need a word with Kate. And, I wouldn't mind seeing Jewel none, either. Break out the soap, boys, and draw me a bath!" Walking toward the house, he added, "I'm calling on a lady!"

U.S. drew back and cringed as Cale murmured, "Jewel?"

To which, U.S. barked, "You heard him! Draw a bath!"

Chapter Eleven

It was about 7:15 in the evening. It would not be full dark for another hour or so, but the sun had dropped below the horizon, and shadows were growing long. Kate was working in the barn when she heard her dogs start to bark. The bitch, which was Jewel's dog, along with her pups were yipping in glee, and Kate dropped a dirty cloth on the workbench and ran outside to see her daughter and Jack riding up the road.

Kate broke into a smile and ran toward the approaching couple. Seeing her ma, Jewel gave her mare a light kick and galloped toward the house. Jack, however, scowled and stayed behind.

Henry was sitting in front of the bunkhouse watching Kate and Jewel's reunion. His eyes narrowed at the sight of Jack Ballard, and he gazed down at the handsome new dousing stick he'd just finished whittling with a wicked-looking Arkansas blade.

Kate cried, "Oh, honey, it's good to see you!" She gave

Jewel a hug and saw her daughter looking at the house, the dilapidated condition of the yard and barn, and the diminished livestock. Kicking a pebble with the toe of her boot, she added, "I've been trying to keep the place going…"

Jewel shook her head, and smiled. "Well, we'd better eat those chickens before they die on us. How's Henry?"

Kate looked over her shoulder at Henry and hollered, "Henry, why don't you make yourself useful and kill us a chicken with that toothpick?"

Then she saw Jack pull his horse close and step down to the ground. She could feel his ill temper coming off him like waves of heat.

"What's the matter…" she started to ask but Jack cut her off.

"I'll settle with you after dinner," he growled. "Only this time it's me doing the talking." Without another word, he plucked up the reins of Jewel's horse and led both animals to the water trough.

Kate raised her eyebrows, and Jewel said, "I'm sorry, Mama. I didn't mean to burst the man's bubble, but I told him we hadn't seen a wild horse in these parts for years. Didn't realize you'd told him different…"

Kate gazed after Jack's receding figure and heaved a sigh. "Oh well, I just thought he might come in useful around here for a week or two. But, if he wants to move on, I guess I can't stop him."

Then she squeezed Jewel's neck again and said, "Let's go in and get supper started, okay? I already made some oven bread, and look… damned if Henry might not catch us the main course!"

Kate's normally dour expression eased into a smirk and then downright laughter, as she and Jewel watched Henry staggering around in a drunken dance, waving his big blade at one of the hens, who was leading him around in a frenzied circle and screaming bloody murder. He bent down to grab the reluctant chicken, but tripped over his own feet and landed, sprawling on the ground in a puff of dust.

Then, as the women watched, the dust cleared, and he held the chicken up in the air with a triumphant shout. "I done it, Kate!" he yelled, and then, "Welcome home, Jewelry!"

As Jack took a much-needed bath, and Kate and Jewel prepared the chicken, pulled out a jar of last year's applesauce, and set the table, Jesse and his sons were tearing through the twilight at a smart trot.

A large, reddish moon was peeking over the hills and U.S. pulled his horse to a stop, jumped off and picked a clutch of yellow, desert paper flowers from the ground. Then he remounted and brought his horse to a run to catch up with the others.

Jesse sat clean and proud in a fancy Mexican-style saddle with a matching bridle and martingale. He wore his best suit; while his sons, in comparison, remained in dusty chaps and floppy Remington hats.

Jesse glanced at the flowers in U.S.'s hands and grinned. "Good thinking, son," he said. Then, he grabbed the flowers out of U.S.'s hand, spurred his fine black gelding into a gallop and headed fast toward the Swain ranch.

———

KATE and her guests were sitting down to dinner. She had asked Jack to say the grace, but he said, "Pass," and bit into a chicken leg.

Henry poured himself another slug of whiskey, and complained, "He's in my place, you know… right at the head of the table! Why?"

Kate snorted. "Because, that's where he belongs." Glancing over at Jewel, she said, "…even if this is his last night with us."

Jack looked to Jewel and understood that she had told Kate about the horses—or the lack thereof. He stared back down at his plate and took a bite of the applesauce and fried peppers.

Kate continued talking to Jewel despite Jack's sullen silence. "And, how's your needlepoint?"

Jack paused on his drumstick and looked up as Jewel sighed. "Well, I wish my lacework were up to my embroidery."

Suddenly they heard hoofbeats approaching fast and close. Jack glanced toward the front door as Kate threw her napkin on the table and exclaimed, "Why, who would be coming up on us at this time of the evening?"

The dogs started to growl, and Jack could hear a peeved-sounding male voice say, "But, Pa! *I* picked them flowers!"

And the response, "Always thinking of your pa, ain't you?"

As Kate stood in the doorway, glaring daggers at the Bolts, Henry said, "Miss Jewel—if I may say so—the embroidery of your personal proportions is second only to those of your lovely mother…"

To which Kate responded, "Any more flattery like that and I'll print my boot on your backside!"

Jack watched as the Bolts stepped up onto the porch and saw a tall, middle-aged man dressed up in 'go to church' clothes, remove his hat and say, "Evenin', Kate."

He was a big man with salt and pepper hair swept back and glued in place with pomade. He held a bouquet of flowers in one big fist. He grinned and said, "I've come to welcome Miss Jewel home."

With that, the Bolt men crowded past Kate, spurs jangling, and walked right up to the dining room table. Kate followed close behind and snapped, "Only one way you'd know she was here… you been spying on me!"

Jesse stopped and stared down at Jewel, stunned by her beauty. He scratched his chin, trying to remember when he'd seen this girl last but only remembered a scruffy, gap-toothed, twelve or thirteen-year-old towhead with twigs in her hair and dirty coveralls on.

The beauty in front of him seemed like a total stranger. Her golden hair was done up and wrapped around her head like a crown. Her wide blue eyes gazed up at him timidly, but with an inner-strength much like his own. He'd come on business, but he was now smitten. He said, "Why, Miss Jewel. I'll be dogged if you ain't growed into some kind of pretty moonbeam…"

Henry took a deep, angry pull off his jug and hooted, "Better keep the door open, Kate. We need all the fresh air we can get!"

Jesse ignored Henry and asked, "You plan on being home from school very long?"

Jewel looked to her mother, and replied, "Well, these aren't exactly the best of times, Mister Bolt. Are they?"

Jesse nodded in agreement, and then glanced down at the flowers in his hand. Holding the bouquet out, he said, "For you. Kinda to welcome you home."

Jewel reached out to take them, but Kate reacted violently. She snatched the flowers out of Jesse's hand and threw them down on top of his boots. "You don't use my daughter for your kind of social call!"

Jesse whirled and glared at Kate, as Jewel whispered, "Ma…"

But Kate hissed, "Keep out of this, Jewel. I know what I'm talking about! And, so does he… ain't that right, Jesse?"

Jesse bent down to pick the flowers up off the floor. Then he tore them to shreds with his big red hands and threw the whole mess on the table and the remaining food. Looking at Kate, his voice was filled with venom. "Kate," he growled. "If you ain't thinking of selling, then you better well plan on moving!'

Kate stood speechless as he continued, "You been offered fifty cents on the acre. Take it. Go on somewhere where there's more water for growing your corn and taters…"

"But," Kate cried, "I've lived here fifteen years! No—I ain't moving…or selling!"

Jesse shrugged and replied, "You better understand, I ain't so generous as to give you a choice."

Jack had heard enough. He gave them all a look—a

look that said he'd been here before, known arguments such as these, and he was sick and tired of it.

Frustrated and swallowing his anger, he stood up, grabbed his pistol and belt, put on his hat and walked past the Bolts and out the front door.

Chapter Twelve

Jack walked outside, heading toward his bunk but paused at the sudden escalation of argument coming from the house. Although he honestly felt like slapping Kate Swain silly, he would never act on his exasperation. But he didn't know if Jesse Bolt, or one of his sons might be moved to violence by that woman's sharp tongue.

Jesse's loud, angry voice rang out in the twilight. "… because come the next long, dry spell my cows is going to have more room for grazing. Next time that river won't be so quick to dry up, either. Because none of you or yours will be around to take your irrigation water from it!"

Kate snapped, "I think that Hiram's got you over a barrel. Is that it, Jesse? Owe him money, do you?"

Jesse said, "I'm giving you one week, Kate. To pack up and be gone. You and all your neighbors, too."

Jack hunkered down beside the puppies, which were taking nourishment from their mother. He heard Jesse add, "It was my mistake letting any of you move in around here in the first place."

Kate replied, "You just try moving me out, Jesse! I'll be the first one to pull the trigger… ain't no one asked to be a part of your problems."

Jesse said, "Then, like the tarantula said to the scorpion —one of us has to lose…"

Kate answered, "No, Jesse. Both of us will lose."

Jack saw Jesse move past the front door and heard him say, "I hope you're back to school again, Jewel. Soon… real soon." And then, "Let's be going, boys."

Jack stepped away from the trees, so he could see the interior of the house. He saw Jesse and his sons putting on their hats but also saw U.S. hesitate in front of Jewel and look her up and down with ravenous eyes. He drawled, "Sure would be a real honor having you at my supper table, Miss Jewel."

Kate stepped in front of her daughter and barked, "You keep your mind off her honor, U.S.! And get the hell outta here!"

U.S. kept his gaze on Jewel and held his hungry, cocky smile for a beat. Then he said, "Be seeing you, Jewel."

Jewel ducked her head, obviously embarrassed. Then, U.S. followed his pa and brothers outside into the night.

––––––––

JACK HAD MOVED from the shadows to keep an eye on the Bolts, and now Jesse stood on the porch staring down at him. His sons crowded around him, and glared at what they considered a strong but barely understood threat.

Jesse said, "Ballard, ain't it?"

Jack nodded. "That's right."

"Well," Jesse said, "If I was you, Ballard, I'd stay in the shade and out of the heat."

Jack made no comment and after a moment, Jesse turned to mount his horse.

The boys made to follow, and Jack said, "Let her be." His voice was soft but came hard to Jesse who hesitated and then turned toward Jack with a scowl.

Jack smiled slightly, adding, "And stay off her land—all of you—from now on."

Jesse snarled, "Don't you hear good? Or maybe you ain't much of a listener…"

Jack answered, "Could be." And then he walked up to where Jesse stood. He wore no gun, but Jesse felt the heat of intent coming off Ballard like a blow.

Jesse's pride made him grit his teeth and say, "Then, that pretty well makes it your problem, don't it?"

By now, Kate, Jewel and Henry had crowded onto the porch. U.S., his own personal pride already stung by Jewel's cold reception, came up to stand beside his pa. He looked down at Jack and sneered, "Oh, he's got shade on his mind all right, Pa. Sweet Jewel there, on his mind. Taking her in the cool shade… imagine that, Pa!"

Wham! Jack's punch sent U.S. reeling backwards right past Kate, Jewel and Henry into the house and clear over the dinner table. The plates, food and silverware crashed onto the floor. Jewel let out a little scream, but Kate started yelling in anger when Cale and Garland rushed Jack.

Jack was too fast for Cale, and he laid down a tattoo of

punches, driving the young man into his horse. Garland, however, had jumped onto Jack's back and hung around his neck like a monkey. Even as Jack drove another fist into Cale's belly, Garland punched Jack hard in the kidney.

Jewel screamed and yelled, "Garland, leave him be!" She started down the steps to try and step between Jack and the two Bolt brothers, but Henry grabbed her arm.

"Whoa there, Jewel. Stay out of it."

The girl stood still but a frustrated tear fell from her eye as she saw Garland land another hard punch to Jack's lower back.

Troy was standing back watching and had just touched the grip of his gun, when his father screamed, "Get in there!" and kicked him in the butt—sending Troy pell-mell forward into Jack.

As Jack struggled with Garland, trying to send him into a tree, Troy stepped in with his pistol in hand and tried to clobber Jack over the head with the grip, but Jack hit him so hard, the boy flew into the corral rails. Two lengths of railing collapsed upon Troy's head.

U.S. had collected his wits by now and came tearing down off the porch with his head down. He bowled into Jack and the two men rolled, punching and spitting like cats in the dust. U.S. concentrated his punches on Jack's kidneys, while Jack dug fast fists into U.S.'s stomach until the younger man could hardly breathe.

Finally, Cale and Garland pulled Jack off U.S. Troy tried for one last blow to Jack's head, but instead got in a painful kick to Ballard's back. Then, they were all back down in the dirt—punching, kicking and, in Troy's case, even getting in a bite or two.

Then, Kate's shrill voice cut through the fray like a knife through soft butter. "All right—that's enough! Tearing up my supper dishes and corral is enough for one night!"

Jack got up, breathing hard. He wiped sweat and blood from his face. Then the other men climbed to their feet—looking to their Pa for a sign of what to do. Jesse nodded and put his hat back on his head. "Okay, boys. Time to head for home."

U.S. suddenly went for a sneak punch at Jack who reacted quickly and decked him in his tracks. As U.S. stared up at the stars, and blew blood and snot from his now broken nose, Kate shook her head in disgust and said, "Jesse, will you please take these pups home and cool 'em off?!"

Jesse stared down at U.S., who was climbing to his feet. "Yeah, for now. I'll go easy on ya, Kate. Cause, they was just getting started."

The Bolts moved to their horses, but U.S. paused and snarled at Jack. "You'll get yours... hear me?"

Jack smirked. "Want some more?"

U.S. clapped his hat on his head, glared, and warned, "You'll get yours... you just wait."

Jack turned to Jesse, who said, "What he's saying is not to expect no little fist-to-cuffs in the dust next time."

Jack nodded. "Any way you want it, Bolt."

Jesse shook his big head and turned to Kate. "You ain't doing yourself no favors by keeping him around here... not even for a week."

Kate replied, "You just worry about me, Jesse."

Jesse slapped his hat on his thigh in frustration. "Dammit! You better stop talking so much and do a little more thinking, woman! Come on, let's go home, boys!"

Then they rode out, thundering close to Jack, who yielded no ground. Finally, they were gone, and the dust of their passage hung still in the night air.

Chapter Thirteen

HENRY STOMPED INSIDE TO FETCH HIS BOTTLE AND KATE and Jewel watched as Jack limped toward the cistern. He worked the pump—once, twice. On the third try, a scant amount of water dribbled out, which he used to rinse the blood off his face.

Inside, Henry shouted, "One week, eh? I'll be ready for 'em… they take no chances with me!"

Kate said. "Henry, will you be quiet?"

Henry, grumbling, came to the doorway to protest but saw Kate watching Jack. He stood silent as Kate said, "As I recall, you wanted to talk to me after supper."

Jack gave no response other than cooling his face with water from the cistern.

Kate tried again. "It's after supper…"

Jack finally looked up at Kate. "Yes ma'am, it surely is."

Kate waited a beat but there was no other response. Finally, she tossed her hands up in the air, shrugged and walked back into the house.

Jewel watched her mother leave in a huff, then picked

Jack's gun belt off the chair he'd left it on and walked over to where he stood, dabbing at his lower lip with the tail of his shirt. She said, "You sure can fight," and handed his gun belt over.

He said nothing, but looked into her eyes as if weighing something in his mind. His expression was neither friendly nor hostile, just cold calculation. After a moment, he reached out and took his gear.

She cleared her throat and asked, "Is this goodnight… or goodbye?"

For a second, Jewel thought he would answer her but in the end, he stared at her, then at the house, and then turned and walked toward the bunkhouse without a word.

Jewel stared after Jack's retreating form and sighed. Then she followed her ma into the house.

———

KATE SAT at the table which had been wiped down. Henry had swept the broken dishes, food and silverware into the corner of the room to be dealt with in the morning and he sat by Kate now, pouring her a double-shot from his own jug of whiskey.

She was without her usual bravado and seemed to be in a grim, almost fearful state of mind. Henry was trying to lighten the mood with his normal bluster. Lifting his drink in the air in a kind of toast, he exclaimed, "How 'bout here's to stickin' it out?"

But Kate was staring at her daughter as Jewel made her way into the kitchen. She said, "Welcome home, honey."

Jewel gave a Kate a look—part anger, part sorrow—and then went to her bedroom and closed the door softly behind her.

Henry tried, again, to lift a toast to the occasion but Kate ignored him, swallowed her drink in one large gulp, got up and walked to her own bedroom.

Henry gazed about the empty room, arm still raised. Then he shrugged, downed his drink and sat listening to the Grandfather clock ticking the fruitless hours away.

———

THE NEXT MORNING Henry awoke with a horrible hangover. He sat on the edge of his cot and saw Jack standing by his bunk. The man's shirt was off, and a small slice of sunlight illuminated a dinner-plate sized, black, blue, red and purple bruise on his back. Even in the scant sunlight, it looked like a serious injury.

Henry heard Jack hiss with pain as he put a clean shirt on, and couldn't help but wince with sympathy. In his long days on this earth, Henry had seen many men like Jack ride into town on the lightning, and leave on the thunder of pain, loss and regret.

For the most part, gunslingers were the very harbinger of doom and Henry had—naturally—put Jack in that category... pistol-packer, gunslinger, trouble on the hoof! But staring over at the much younger man who was seated on the edge of his cot, painfully pulling on his boots and not uttering a word of complaint, Henry had to admit that, so far, Jack seemed to be the victim here.

Henry knew Kate. Yes, he did. She was headstrong, relentless and would do just about anything to keep the

Swain ranch going. He would have been happy enough leaving this ranch and all its troubles behind—if only Kate would leave with him, but he knew that as long as Kate insisted on staying, so would he.

Jack, however, had ridden in innocently enough, looking for honest work. It was Kate, and her lies that had prompted this man to stay and get kicked around for doing so.

Jack glanced his way and Henry rose with a groan, holding his aching head. Then he stumbled outside to ease his hangover with cool water from the cistern. Getting very little out of the pump, he tried again and heard Kate say, "Seen Jack this morning?"

Henry, despite his momentary sympathy, was tired of Kate's interest in the gunslinger. He grimaced and looked toward the barn where Jack's buckskin was saddled and waiting. The barn door was open.

Kate turned on her heel and strode toward the barn. Henry shrugged in disgust and bent to attend to his hangover with the scant water available to him.

Inside the barn Jack was standing in front of a once elaborate but now dusty and dilapidated still. His fingers were tracing the outlandish contraption in admiration. It was a machine built of pipes, barrels, pulleys and gears. There was a makeshift drill cable attached to it, a one-cylinder steam engine and a boiler.

Jack didn't know much about rigs like this, but he thought that this machine was pieced together with pirated parts into something other than a whiskey still. He ran his hands over it and was filled with admiration for inventors in general. Then, he heard footsteps behind him. He turned slightly, saw that it was Kate and said, "Building yourself a well driller, are you?"

Brightening, Kate said, "Like you can see, me and Charlie had ourselves a little still here—until water got to be more important than whiskey. After Charlie… left, I started building this well-driller." She gazed up at Jack with interest. "You know something about running one of these?"

Jack frowned, looked her over good and then and walked out of the barn. He said, "You got to build one first."

She followed him outside and said, "Jack, stop!" He stopped walking and turned to face her.

She said, "Reckon we kind of saved our talk for this morning, ain't we?"

Jack moved again as if to keep walking and Kate cried out, "I know Jewel told you there ain't no horses…"

Jack said, "Just who the hell do you think you are? Taking up my time with your trouble and lies!" He walked toward his waiting horse and Kate ran after him.

She asked, "You leaving now?"

Jack turned to face her. "Arguments over land? They somehow always lead to killing, Kate."

Kate's eyes narrowed. "You know all about that, do you? You an expert on that?" Then, as if she wished she could swallow her own hasty words, she clapped a hand over her own mouth and gazed at the ground beneath her feet.

Jack asked, real softly. "Is that what you and Jesse really want, Kate?"

Not answering him, Kate asked instead, "Does that mean you're leaving, or staying?"

Jack mounted his horse and stared down at this vulnerable, proud woman and shook his head. "Let me tell you… you are the most… ornery, most conniving, blustering, bluffin', lying woman I have ever known!"

Kate stared up at him and grinned. She said, "Forget the flattery, and give me an answer, Jack!"

Jack stared at the ranch, the starving livestock and clean laundry on a clothesline, already turning brown with dust. Shaking his head, he said, "Kate, I only know one way of settling arguments."

She followed his gaze and sighed. Then, as he tapped his horse's reins she said, "Hold on! Where you going?"

He pressed his rowels softly into his horse's ribs and said, "To work."

Kate smiled, but he stopped and turned around. Facing her, serious now, he added, "But it could be your bad mistake…" He turned his horse and galloped away.

Chapter Fourteen

JACK RODE SLOWLY, TAKING IN WHAT LANDSCAPE HE COULD through the rising winds. He saw no cattle, only buzzards spinning circles in the sky. He had filled his saddle bags with fence mending tools; wire cutters, a hammer, iron staples and a tightly-wound loop of razor-wire. It was wrapped in an old piece of deer hide to keep the sharp ends from scratching his horse's belly. He planned on fixing the damage U.S. had started to inflict on Kate's fence line when he'd showed up to ruin the man's fun.

He was trying to figure out why he had chosen to stay. He did not trust Kate Swain. Women like her had a habit of getting those around her either hurt or killed. He knew what she wanted; to keep her ranch intact at all costs, and he thought she was willing to sacrifice anything or anyone to keep her dream alive. She couldn't even conceive of a new, softer life—a life that wasn't on the verge of drying up and blowing away.

He was attracted to Jewel Swain, he acknowledged… her bright blue eyes, her fresh face, her long blonde hair.

But she was too young for him… not even twenty-years-old, compared to his thirty-four years. Also, Kate was her mother. The thought of being forever tied to that woman as his mother-in-law was enough to make Jack want to ride away like the devil was on his tail.

There were prettier, and easier women around than Jewel Swain. He knew at least three women who would open their arms to him in a half-dozen towns in Texas, alone. Pretty Martha Landry, a high-priced whore with long black hair and grass green eyes. Martha had enough clout in the brothel she worked to clear her calendar whenever Jack rode into town.

And, Jennifer Townsend. A rich married woman whose husband was far too old to attend her voracious needs. Seventy-five miles north, and Jack would find himself in her soft, tawny embrace and silken sheets.

Then, there was Sally Owens with her curly red hair and bright brown eyes. The orphaned daughter of a notorious outlaw, Sally had dedicated her adult life to upholding the law, and was one of the few female deputies in Texas. The problem with Sally was that she was in love with Jack, who was in no way ready to settle down and lie in a marriage bed for the rest of his life.

No, it wasn't any kind of affection or physical attraction that kept him from leaving the Swain ranch. It was… pity, maybe, or resentment at how the strong so often vanquished the weak. He knew that the minute he rode off, the Bolts would lay waste to Kate and her daughter's ranch. U.S. would have his way with Jewel whether she wanted it or not, and Jesse would probably throttle Kate to death to keep from hearing her squawk.

Jack felt a shudder tickle the back of his neck. Pulling

his horse up short, he laid his hand on the butt of his carbine, and looked around. Gazing into the distance he saw nothing but heat shimmering up from the scorched ground. Dust was everywhere in a reddish, gray haze. He blinked and saw a pair of riders emerge from the heat shimmers. They were riding parallel to him. Then, a sudden gust of dust-laden wind hid the men from his eyes.

Jack pulled his carbine from the sheath, peered down the barrel of his rifle through the sights and panned the landscape, but the riders had disappeared. He sheathed the gun, shrugged his disquiet away and brought his gelding up to a smart trot.

He rode a couple of miles and looking ahead, saw that the two tall posts that separated the Bolt ranch from the Swain ranch were now reduced to only one. The post hung with the Bolt brand was still standing tall, but the post that announced Kate's property had been sawed off and lay flat on the ground amid a pile of razor wire. Looking further, Jack saw that the fencing he'd come to repair was also gone… at least 500 feet of it. Only the post holes remained, and those were rapidly filling with dust and sand.

Jack looked across the land, the long line of empty post holes, the broken signs, and the bones of the calf which had been picked clean by the buzzards. Pressing his heels into his horse's flanks, he rode forward a few paces and looked down at Charlie Swain's grave marker.

It too had been broken at ground level and lay flat on the ground. Tumbleweeds had blown over the slight depression and Jack read the words etched into the wood slats-

Charlie Swain
1828-1878
He Owned Land

ABRUPTLY, Jack knew why he was staying. It wasn't lust or a sense of honor, but rage. It was one thing… moving a fence line, but quite another vandalizing a man's grave. That showed cruel, frightening intent.

Jack had seen this sort of thing happen one too many times, and he knew that if he didn't stay, not only would Kate and Jewel lose their ranch, it was more than likely they would lose their lives, as well.

He clicked his tongue to ride for home, but his gaze suddenly swiveled to the right. The same two riders sat their horses in the distance on Bolt land. They weren't moving—just standing in the heat shimmers. Then, Jack watched as the dust rose once more, and the riders disappeared into the haze like spirits.

————

HENRY WAS a half mile away from the ranch house, walking along a dried-up creek bed. He believed that a good water-witch investigated the lands *natural* vulnerability to water before anything else. River beds, spring pools, large areas of brush—were all signs that water almost always navigated from the earth's deepest aquifers to these tender spots on the surface, despite weather conditions.

He was thinking about his ma, pa and uncle Timothy —all gone these many years. Henry's father, Clive, was a traveling preacher. He and his family had traveled the back roads of Texas, Oklahoma, New Mexico and Nevada preaching "Hellfire and Brimstone" for many years before finally succumbing to an Comanche Indian attack in North Texas, when Henry was twelve-years-old.

The only reason Henry had survived the attack was because he was following his uncle Tim—a well-meaning but slow fellow in his late twenties. Tim had been born with his ma's birthing cord pulled taut around his neck and had almost strangled to death before the midwife could cut the cord. Baby Timmy had survived the ordeal but had grown up to be a little simple in the head.

Although Tim couldn't read or write and could barely remember from one day to the next how to tie his own shoes, he was a wizard at witching for water. Although Henry loved his ma and pa, and tried to be a good, "God-Fearing" son, his bigger fascination was watching as his uncle brought water up out of parched earth. It was some sort of magic, and like a sorcerer's apprentice, Henry wanted his uncle to teach him how to harness those mystical powers.

They were about 600-yards away from the family wagon that fateful day, hunkered down over a gravelly piece of soil and watching a wet patch grow larger and larger after Tim's dowsing stick had suddenly jerked down toward the ground as if a big trout had just taken the bait off a fishing line.

Suddenly, the man and boy heard Indian war cries

sounding over the prairie. Tim made the mistake of standing up to see what was going on, and was immediately spotted by the war-party but Henry, already hidden by a large clump of brush, dove under the weeds and waited for death to come.

It was the most difficult thing he'd ever had to do or would ever be forced to do again. He heard an arrow strike his uncle's chest and saw him fall close to the tumbleweeds he hid beneath. Then, Henry heard the thunder of unshod hooves approach and had to watch as the Comanches slit his uncle's throat and took his scalp as a prize.

Henry thought that his folks had perished by now as well, so he sat quiet as a mouse and hoped the Indians' keen eyes wouldn't spot him. He saw many moccasined feet milling about, and then, just as they were mounting up to ride away, Henry watched as a light brown scorpion unfurled its long stinger, and sank it into his bare ankle.

Henry almost screamed out loud at the pain, but managed to keep his mouth shut as the marauding Indians rode away, triumphant. The scorpion went on its merry way and after about an hour, Henry crawled out from under the brush. His ankle was the size of a cantaloupe, and hot to the touch, but he knew that the scorpions sting, although horribly painful, would not kill him.

He had sat for the rest of that day and night, shaking with fear and fever and watched as flies covered his ma and pa's bodies. He knew that, as sick as he was, there was no way he could bury his relatives; so finally, he got up and started hobbling toward the next town for help.

Henry survived the intervening years—first at an

orphanage, then as the ward of an elderly couple in Nebraska who were in need of a farmhand. Later, after the old folks had passed on, he joined the Confederate Army, and then thrived for a while as a gambler of some repute. But, always, he had held respect and admiration for water wizards—those wild-eyed, unsung heroes of droughts, everywhere.

His face held that furor now. Just a few minutes ago, his new dousing stick had suddenly dipped toward the ground, much like Uncle Tim's had done so many years earlier. Henry's heart soared. *Just imagine Kate's smile if I can uncover the Earth's bounty in the form of cool, clean water!* he thought.

Holding his stick straight out in front of him, Henry prayed, "Listen here, Lord. I don't mind you shining all this light down on me. But, why be so stingy with all that water we know you got hidden under me?"

Henry held his arms out so stiff they began to ache, and sweat ran down his forehead in sheets. He was about to begin a new prayer when he heard hoof beats approaching. Unfortunately, his memories of that long-ago Indian attack meshed with reality, and he whirled around to face the approaching savages.

He waved his divining stick in the air, and yelled, "Stay back, you! You just beat tar!" Then, peering through the heat waves, Henry saw that it was Jack Ballard walking up slowly on his horse.

Henry glared. "I don't appreciate the interruption!"

Jack pulled his horse to a stop. Looking down at the scrawny little man and seeing his flushed face and sweat-covered torso, he took a canteen off his saddle horn and offered it to Henry. "Care for a drink?" he asked.

Henry scowled. "I'll find my own, thank you."

Looking skeptical, Jack said, "Oh, you will, will you?"

Henry watched Jack take a deep drink and his Adam's apple quivered in longing. He growled, "I got work to do, you know, searching out that impermeable analogy to running river water…"

Jack listened and then took another deep draught.

Henry drew himself up and continued, "A water vein is likely to follow beneath hollows or depressions or folding of the strata…

Holding out the canteen again, Jack said, "You really believe in that stick, don't you?"

Offended, Henry stamped his foot on the ground. Raising the stick up in the air, Henry shouted, "You do things your way and I'll handle 'em my way… understand?"

Jack grinned and raised one hand in mocking surrender.

Henry added, "I can do more for Kate with this stick than you could ever accomplish with that piece of iron you carry!"

Fed up with the little man's contempt, Jack answered, "Well, I can prove what I do… what about you?"

Too thirsty to pursue his argument, Henry grabbed the canteen out of Jack's hand and swallowed a great mouthful of water. He attempted to take on Jack's gaze, but lost his will and grumbled, "Yeah, you're proving it all right! It was your idea, wasn't it?"

Jack frowned, "You mean, about me staying on?"

But Henry shook his shaggy black and gray mane and shouted, "Kate's big shindig! Bringing the neighbors over… well, she can damn well count me out! I won't be a part of her war-party!"

Jack took a step backward, shook his head in amazement, mounted up and rode away, leaving Henry alone with the realization that Jack was just as surprised and dismayed as *he* had been at hearing about Kate's newest scheme.

Chapter Fifteen

KATE HAD SPENT THE MORNING RIDING JEWEL'S MARE TO her friendliest neighbors. She handed out party invitations and told all her friends that a new man named Jack Ballard had taken up residence at the Swain ranch. She also hinted, heavily, that there might be more than casual interest between Jack and her daughter, Jewel.

She informed everyone that they were going to kill a steer, and roast the rest of her chickens for a party to take place the next day. A shindig in honor of Jewel's return from school, and a generous toast of whiskey for everyone in vicinity who shared in the droughts punishment.

There were eight small homesteads and two sizable ranches bordering the Swain ranch, and every parched and starving owner smiled at her invite and swore they would be more than happy to attend.

Kate rode for home by mid-afternoon and was well satisfied. *Now*, she thought, *I just need someone to kill one of the cows and help me slaughter the rest of my chickens.*

Setting up the party for the following day was reckless but necessary. She knew from Henry's reaction that her idea would be poorly received by Jack. Even Jewel seemed appalled at the idea of some big fuss made over her homecoming. What's more; Jewel knew Kate well, and had accused her mother of some sort of hidden agenda.

Kate snorted as she rode for home. *So, what?* she thought. *No one else is going to save us from the Bolts, so I might as well bring in some reinforcements—especially since Jesse made it clear that he not only wants me gone, but all my neighbors as well.*

She figured that once she had all her friends and neighbors gathered in one spot (her front yard) and plied them with good victuals and whiskey, they would see reason and join with her against the Bolts.

Why, that would be… She added them up in her mind… *almost twenty men, fifteen women and another six kids! An army!* She smiled with satisfaction and mentally rubbed her hands together with glee.

Still… her mood darkened. Henry's reaction had been emphatic and wholly unfriendly. Kate knew the man was besotted with her and although she did not share in his affection, his criticism of her idea had stung. Shrugging in resentment, she uttered, "So what if that *water witch* ain't keen on my idea? What does his opinion matter to me?"

Looking toward her ranch, she realized something, however. Henry's opinion of her *had* come to matter. Since he had decided to stay at her ranch after Charlie took the easy road out, his small but sturdy presence had become a fixture—both for her and Jewel. Sure—he drank like a fish but so had Charlie. So did she, for that matter, at least when times were good.

The withering look he'd given her this morning after she shared her idea with him had scared her a little, and she realized that she'd begun to lean on the man, both for masculine support and as a close friend—a friend whose opinion mattered.

She sighed. *Enough of that!* she decided. *If Henry Chase doesn't like it, he can just high-tail it on outta here.*

Thus fortified, she kicked the little mare up to a gallop and headed for home. She had some whiskey to un-cask and chickens to kill.

———

A COUPLE HOURS LATER, Kate stood in front of Jack in the barn. She had already killed her chickens—all but two of her best layers—and had just finished draining most of her remaining whiskey into eight glass jugs for the party to come.

Although she had been prepared for Jack's displeasure she felt a bit intimidated by the young man looming over her. *He really does look like the worst sort of storm cloud when he's mad!* she thought.

Not one to back down, though, she turned away from Jack's wrath and started fiddling with her well-drilling contraption. Unfortunately, she touched the wrong piece of apparatus, and the whole thing came crashing down on the floor of the barn. A huge plume of dust set the bats in the loft to squeaking and soaring throughout the building and out the upstairs windows.

Coughing and waving her hands in the air to clear away the dust, Kate looked for Jack to finish her point, but he was gone. Hurrying outside, she saw him dip a ladle into the water trough and stare at her sideways as she walked up. Looking past Jack, Kate also saw Henry standing close by. Both men were staring at her with sullen, angry eyes.

Frustrated at this unexpected show of masculine solidarity, Kate puffed herself up and stamped her foot in the dirt. Pointing at Henry, she said, "I don't care what *he* told you! It's Jewel's party. She needs it—she deserves it!"

Jack lifted an eyebrow, and Henry shook his head in disgust.

Thoroughly incensed by now, Kate yelled, "And so do my neighbors, dammit! So, you two get to work helping me. I need someone to kill a steer and help me pluck the chickens for tomorrow night's party. And get yourselves spruced up for the shindig. It's about time Jewel's fiancé met our neighbors!"

She crossed her arms over her breasts, and grinned. "Yessir, Jack. Having us a social!"

Then she gave the younger man an impudent stare but wilted as he said, "You better have your fun now, Kate." His expression was not angry but grave. "They tore down your fence line… every post and strand of it."

Kate's eyes filled with tears as Jack added, "That means you and Jesse got more than an argument to settle now."

Chapter Sixteen

As Jack took the wagon and his carbine out to shoot a steer, and Henry set to dipping Kate's dead chickens in a vat of boiling water, another small drama was playing out nineteen miles away in a dusty crossroad enclave about a mile and a half away from town.

Two wagon trails intersected at one of the last surviving concerns in this parched and lonely part of Texas. If you were riding east toward town, you would stumble upon a small adobe bank (The Bank of Brazos), the Brazos Water and Feed Company, and The Pearly Gates Hotel and Casino.

All these businesses were owned by Hiram Flint who sat now at the bar of his hotel with old, Pete Tremaine— the barkeep, Floyd Little—the Faro and Poker dealer and Jean Smalley—the manager (and, if you were to split straws—Madam) of The Pearly Gates Hotel.

Three young women lounged in the drawing room, just off the bar area. Two of the girls were still attractive, but the oldest of the whores was scarred from an early case of the pox. She had wild and ratty brown hair and a jaundiced, wandering eye which gave her the look of a deranged barn owl.

Anna Cline (or Owley, as she was known) studied her counterparts and snorted. "What gives you the idea that you are too good to do the laundry?" she demanded of Conchita Perez, who stared back at her with dark, flashing eyes.

The daughter of a Mexican prostitute and a Comanche brave, Conchita had run away from her abusive parents and lived on the streets of Mexico City as a beggar and a whore since she was eleven-years-old. She considered being asked to come and work for Hiram Flint when she was seventeen a blessing and now, at twenty-years-old she still had her dark, good looks and all her teeth which she knew would have been punched out of her mouth had she stayed at home with her drunken, violent mother and father.

She was normally an ally to her sisters-in-arms but today she hissed like a snake,

"Meester Flint, thas who! He say to keep myself pretty for a special guest coming today!" she answered, and tossed her long curtain of black hair at Owley with a sniff.

"Well," Owley asked the other whore, "what's *your* excuse?"

Trudy Powers smiled. "Same for me, Owley. Flint said to be ready for a high paying guest and to keep myself fresh and clean, but he won't be coming until later. How 'bout if I help you wash the laundry, but you finish with the hanging up?"

Trudy was the prettiest young woman in the room, with light brown hair and large blue eyes. She had stumbled upon prostitution quite by accident when she'd shipped out on a wagon train a few years earlier with a half-dozen other women as a "Mail-Order Bride".

Their wagon had arrived in Houston as scheduled but when her traveling companions disappeared like smoke as their new husbands arrived to pick them up, Trudy stood alone as the wagon train departed. She stayed alone, waiting for a certain Mr. Williams to show up and claim her, but after two days she prepared to catch a train back to Virginia.

Three hours before the train arrived, she saw a wagon approaching and the driver-a skinny man wearing a checkered vest and a bowler hat introduced himself as Travis Williams—her husband to be. Relieved, although rather unimpressed by the looks of her prospective groom, Trudy climbed aboard the wagon and set off to make the best of her new life in Texas.

Little did she know, she had just been tricked by an unscrupulous character named Civil Carruthers who had seen this sort of thing happen before and knew how to make a profit off these girls' predicaments. Within eight hours of being picked up and lied to by Carruthers, Trudy was in a back-alley bar on an auction block, being sold as a prostitute to the highest bidder.

She, too, considered herself lucky to have been purchased by Hiram Flint. The accommodations were adequate, the Madam; Jean Smalley was remote but kind enough, and the girls had regular access to decent food and the local doctor whenever they needed one. Hiram Flint seemed to be a cold fish, but he never allowed his working girls to be harmed by their clients. The pay-share was pretty good, too. Trudy had managed to set away over two hundred dollars for her eventual escape into a better life—whenever and whatever that might be.

But, special orders were rare, and Trudy had no intention of getting herself all hot and sweaty when she'd been told to stay fresh and clean for a "special guest".

Still, she felt bad for Owley who almost always got the short end of the stick when it came to manual labor. She also got the worst-looking, stinkiest and nastiest clients, all because smallpox had come to visit when she was just a baby. So, Trudy tried to show as much respect and affection toward Anna as possible.

Owley glared for a few seconds and then came over to give Trudy a hug. "You are a good girl, Trudy. Thank you."

Suddenly, the girls heard the front screen door screech open and the murmur of masculine voices. All three froze for a second and then ran to peek through a hole in the adobe wall at the man who had just arrived. Neither Trudy or Conchita knew who their particular "guest" might be so the women studied the newcomer carefully.

Trudy felt a cold shudder run through her veins as she studied the stranger's profile. He was an angular man; pale, deadly, and malevolent. His skin was the gray and golden brown of a rattlesnake's hide, and his eyes were icy green. He wore two guns; long barrels—one with the grip forward and the other gun in the traditional manner, hip-high.

Trudy found herself hoping that this man would be Conchita's *guest* for the afternoon. Not that she wished any harm on the girl but her heart was filled with dread at the sight of him. She had no doubt that the man was a hired gun and had come to these parts to inflict as much damage as he could.

All three women heard the man say, "You sent for me?"

Mr. Flint hesitated while looking the man up and down. Then he asked, "You Bob Trey? Out of Waco?"

Trey returned Flint's gaze and turned to look around at this windswept, God Forsaken little crossroads. Then he took his hat off and sat down at a table closest to the one window in the bar. He nodded in answer to Hiram's question, and Flint said, "Then, I sent for you."

"I'm here." Trey said.

Trudy saw a small, slow smile cross Flint's face.

Unfortunately, it was *her* misfortune to be assigned to Bob Trey for the duration of his stay and from then on, she was never the same. The brave young woman who had come to Texas as a mail-order bride, who was tricked and sold into prostitution but had managed to smile and cling to the hope of a better life died the first night Bob Trey took to her bed.

He was silent in his sexual torture, and deadly.

Four and a half months later, filled with unrelenting self-loathing and shame, Trudy Powers took her own life.

Chapter Seventeen

JEWEL SAT ON THE EDGE OF HER BED IN A BRIGHT SLASH OF sunshine and picked the stitches out of the waistline of one of her old dresses. The dress was a red and black Madras plaid, and had once been one of her favorites but it was faded now to a dull pink and gray and the hemline was halfway up her shins… far too short for what passed as fashionable in this part of Texas.

Still, her mother had knocked on Jewel's bedroom door earlier and asked if she could alter one of her dresses for Kate to wear at the party. Jewel was so shocked by the request, she could only stare, google-eyed. She could not remember seeing her mother wear a dress—ever.

Her mouth must have been hanging open, because after seeing her daughter's shocked expression, Kate had grinned and said, "You're going to catch a fly, ya know." And then, blushing, she added, "How do you expect me to sway the neighbors in their thinking if I don't look no better'n a farmhand? I don't normally like to a wear a dress if I can help it, but this is too important for me to take a half-way measure."

Jewel had shown her mother what dresses she had hanging in her closet, and Kate had chosen the old plaid. Which was fine by Jewel, but Kate did not boast a 26-inch waist. Which was why she was altering it to fit Kate's shorter, stouter frame.

Bringing the waistline out to a more reasonable 32-inches, Jewel scrutinized her handiwork, and nodded in satisfaction. *This will do*, she thought. Then, she laid the garment on the bed and stared at herself in the cracked and dusty mirror on the wall.

Long blonde hair, blue eyes, pretty, clear skin... *So, why does Jack not see what I have to offer?* she wondered. *Is it my age?*

Why, her best friend Beatrice had just married a man twice her age and at seventeen, she was two years younger than Jewel! Maybe Jack already had a sweetheart stashed back home from where he came. She shook her head in teenaged despair.

The only boy she had ever looked at twice was the brother of one of her schoolmates, who had shown an interest in her. His name was Leonard Adams, and although he had piqued her interest, somewhat, he paled in comparison to Jack Ballard with his large bobbing Adam's Apple, bulbous brown eyes, and acne-ridden complexion.

Comparing Jack's visage to Leonard's was well... depressing. Jack was tall for one thing, and as strong as an oak tree. His reddish-brown hair was thick and shiny, and his smoky hazel eyes made Jewel's heart pound with excitement, and her knees quiver with longing.

"Oh!" Jewel sighed and turned to gaze at the dress she had set out to wear tonight. It was her newest and best dress; the dress she had won the champion ribbon for at her school's sewing competition. It was blue satin, with pale yellow and pink flowers embroidered on the low-cut bodice. She had only worn it once for the competition at school, and she knew she looked beautiful in it. Jewel couldn't help but wonder if Jack would think so too.

Standing up with an exasperated click of her teeth, Jewel headed out to the kitchen to help her mother prepare beans, bread, spuds and a barbecue sauce for tonight's dinner party.

———

A FEW HOURS LATER, as Jewel and her mother shared a tub of warm bath water, (Jewel went first since Kate, as usual, was as dirty as the men) and Jack and Henry lugged long, plank-style tables out to the front yard from the back of the barn, Troy and Garland sat their horses on their favorite high, hidden bluff and watched as one wagon after another rolled across the prairie towards Kate's ranch.

They could see that most of these folks were dressed up in their "Sunday go-to-Meeting" clothes and they could actually smell the fragrance of sweet breads and pastries wafting up in the air from the back of their wagons. Kate was throwing a party!

Looking toward each other, the Bolt brothers decided that this news needed to reach U.S.'s ears as soon as possible. Kate Swain on her own was no clear threat, they knew, but getting the whole neighborhood involved could pose more problems than the Bolts could handle.

Setting their rowels to use, Troy and Garland flew toward the Bolt Lightning ranch. Arriving a few minutes later, they saw U.S. and Cale stacking bales of hay by the horse pasture. Garland noticed the foul expression on his big brother's face and knew he and Troy were in trouble for bugging out on the daily chores. He figured U.S. would make them pay for their truancy, but right now he had news to share.

"U.S.! Kate's having herself a party! We seen a bunch of riders and wagons headed over to her ranch filled with good food and lots of people!"

U.S. *was* ticked off at his two brothers, but perked up at Garland's news. *A party, eh? Who can afford to throw a shindig these days? Not Kate Swain, for sure.*

Glancing toward the house, his eyes narrowed in speculation. Jesse was heading over to Flint's whorehouse—the horny old goat. And he was, even now, using up their hard-bought water rations to get all spiffed up... again!

U.S. was heartily sick of it, especially since his father suddenly had a bee in his bonnet for U.S.'s own girl, Jewel! He gritted his teeth, and turning to his brothers said, "Don't tell father what you seen, boys. That'll be our little secret. Keep it quiet, and maybe I won't thrash both of you for skipping out on your chores!"

Troy, Garland and Cale nodded obediently and went to work helping U.S. stack the rest of the hay.

Chapter Eighteen

U.S. THOUGHT ABOUT THINGS FOR A LITTLE WHILE AND then walked in on his father's bath. He informed Jesse that a bunch of neighbors were gathering at Kate's house for a party, and he told his pa what he thought he and his brothers should do about it.

Jesse, after getting over his anger at being so rudely interrupted in his toilette sank back in the sudsy water and mulled over U.S.'s suggestion. A moment later, he smiled and said, "Okay—you do that. But, U.S.…. I don't want no bloodshed, okay? This is just to give 'em a scare. That's all."

U.S. nodded silently and left Jesse to rally his brothers for some fun. They outfitted their mounts with all the equipment they might need to carry out their mischief and waited for their father to appear before setting out on their evening task.

Finally, Jesse appeared wearing his best gray suit and a new Derby hat. He had even plucked a red poppy from behind the house and pinned it to his hatband. It was all

U.S. could do to keep from rolling his eyes in disgust. Jesse walked along the verandah toward his waiting wagon and the team that was hitched and ready to go. In the back of the wagon sat several empty water barrels.

Jesse glanced at his sons and said, "I'll be back tomorrow, and bring back more water and hay. You all go out and do what we agreed on and don't get caught."

Staring at his oldest boy, Jesse added, "Remember U.S., leave Kate and Ballard for tomorrow—when I get back. Don't go off half-cocked and do something stupid, okay?"

U.S. replied, "We know what to do."

Jesse stared U.S. down and frowned. There was something about the look in his oldest son's eyes that set a tickle of distrust up and down his spine. He was about to quiz his boys as to what they were up to, but U.S. gave him a confident, toothy grin.

"We'll do the job right, Pa. Don't worry about it."

Giving his offspring one final glance, Jesse snapped the long reins over his horse's backs and the wagon rattled down the road and out of sight. The boys waited for about ten minutes to make sure their father wasn't going to change his mind and turn back for home. Then, U.S. said, "Let's ride, boys!"

The Bolt brothers rode in a large circle and approached a bluff where they could look down on Kate's house and still be fairly well hidden in the darkening shadows. U.S. had "borrowed" his father's telescope and he glassed the front yard and stable area of the Swain ranch.

"Whatcha see, U.S.?" Garland said, trying to peer over his brother's shoulder at the front of Kate's home. "Is she really having a party?"

U.S. grunted in the affirmative, and Cale scoffed, "Well, of course she is, Garland. Can't you just smell that beef barbecue? And, listen to the music!"

U.S., meanwhile, had taken the opportunity to search for Jewel in the crowd of people gathered under the cottonwood trees, and by the bonfire. His heart almost stopped when he saw her standing close to the gun slinger, Jack Ballard.

She was a vision… an angel come down to earth in her shiny blue dress, but he noticed that she only had eyes for the man who was fixing to cut into a hunk of beef roast. U.S.'s heart turned to stone as he eavesdropped on her adoration. Jewel had never gazed at him with that look in her eyes! *What does the pistol-packer have that I don't?* he wondered in dismay.

"U.S.! What do you want to do?" Troy interrupted his thoughts. "Do you wanna crash that shindig?"

For a moment, U.S. was tempted. Their sudden appearance would certainly throw a wrench in the works, wouldn't it? But, no. There looked to be, at least, twenty armed men at the party. He and his brothers might just be too good of a target for those men to ignore.

U.S. thought about it for a moment and then he turned his horse around and grinned at his siblings. "Nah, we'll do what pa wants, I reckon."

Cale, noticing the evil look in his brother's eyes asked, "What… what are we a gonna do?"

U.S. winked and said, "Let's go calling on the neighbors!"

His brothers stared at him for a second and then smiled and followed him around a stony outcropping and down to the wagon trail leading to the Swain ranch's neighbors.

———

WAGONS AND HORSES were parked in front of Kate's stable and people milled around under a big stand of trees and hovered over the whiskey punch bowl.

Two fiddle players, Randall Hughes and his sister Gertie played ballads by the corral rails, and there was a small reception line hosted by Kate and Jewel. Most of the visitors took their turn showing off their offerings— cakes, biscuits, salads and what vegetables had survived the drought—and welcoming Jewel home.

Kate, looking very nice but uncomfortable in her borrowed finery, welcomed her guests with pride and a certain anxious excitement. *This could be it!* she thought. *The one sure-fire way to beat the Bolts at their own game!*

She said, "Why, thank you, Coleen! It's really Jewel's dress. She... enlarged it, slightly."

Then, turning to Jewel, she asked, "Jewel, you know Harold and Coleen Enders, right?"

Jewel smiled and said, "I sure do. How nice seeing you here!" Then, she exclaimed, "Luke and Belle Clayton... hello! Welcome to our little party!"

Kate raised her voice enough to be heard by all. "Everybody..." she pointed at Jack who was starting to carve the thin, tough beef into strips. "That man setting to on the roast? That's Jack Ballard. Get to know him, because he's my man around here!"

Jack looked up at Kate with a slight frown, and commenced to carving the beef.

Kate continued her introduction. "You all should know… you all should know that Jack's a professional well driller!"

A whisper of excitement ran through the crowd, and Kate smiled. "That's right," she continued. "He come clear from Nebraska to help us out."

Jewel blushed at her mother's lie and stared at the ground beneath her feet, as Jack stopped carving the beef and gave Kate a scowl. The crowd, however, broke into spontaneous applause at hearing about his line of work.

Jack, himself, was starting to blush when Kate said in a confidential tone of voice; "Mind you, I ain't giving away none of Jewel's secrets, but…"

Jack stood up straight and stared at Jewel who was gazing back at him with bold, excited eyes, "but, she and Jack is love birds!"

There was another ripple of titillated interest throughout the crowd as Jack studied Jewel's face and saw that, despite Kate's outlandish lies, there was more truth in her mother's statement—at least as far as Jewel was concerned, than he had realized.

Chapter Nineteen

JESSE PULLED UP AT A CROSSROAD. ONE TRACK HEADED INTO town… such as it was now that the drought had driven off most folks, and the businesses they had once owned and operated with pride. The other track led toward Flint's operation—the Bank of Brazos with its predatory interest rates, the Brazos Water and Feed Company with its exorbitantly priced water and grain, and the Pearly Gates Hotel and Casino, with it's low-end but high-priced prostitutes.

A half an hour later, he pulled his wagon around in front of the feed barn and saw that he seemed to be the only customer. Jesse frowned at the glow of light coming from the bank's front window, stepped down off the wagon, tied his horses to a post and walked over to the bank.

He knocked on the door, but getting no response tried the doorknob and walked inside. Looking around, Jesse took note of the condition of this once prosperous establishment. Most of the gilt paint Flint had used to decorate the two tellers' cages was peeling onto the floor. The couch and matching easy chairs furnishing the lobby were gone as well, giving the room the sad, lonesome feel of a haunted house.

Jesse moved toward the back room where a lantern burned fitfully in a wall sconce. He saw Hiram Flint standing behind his desk, and thought that the man looked even smaller and skinnier than he had a week earlier. The lantern light cast Flint's gaunt face in eerie shadows making it look like a floating skull.

Jesse snorted. *Appropriate,* he thought. *A spook to run the ghost house!*

Hiram glanced at Jesse and said, "I trust you came with good news?"

Jesse felt his anger rise at the insolence in Flint's voice. He took a deep breath and studied a large map of West Texas tacked to the wall behind Flint's desk. Looking closer, he also saw a large circle of red, flagged pins that he knew encompassed his Bolt Lightning ranch, Swain's Cattle Company ranch and almost all the other, smaller ranches within fifty square miles of where he currently stood.

Although, in his heart, Jesse had known he was risking his own property when he signed up on Hiram's nefarious schemes, seeing his beloved ranch trapped inside those red pins made his heart pound with dread. Palms clammy with sweat, Jesse said, "Well, hello to you, too, Hiram. I come for a steak dinner and a little… companionship."

Flint shrugged. "You'll have to talk to Pete about that steak, but Trudy ain't available tonight. You'll have to make do with Conchita."

"Why?" Jesse barked. "You know I like Trudy!"

"Sorry, she taken right now." Then he glared, and said, "The clock is ticking, Jesse. Have you gotten rid of those small-timers, yet?"

Jesse who'd had his mind set on spending the night in Trudy's arms, grumbled, "It's being done right now."

Hiram nodded. "How 'bout Kate? She's gotta go too…"

Jesse said, "I'm handling her personally. Tomorrow."

Flint abruptly turned toward the wall and put on his suit coat, "We can't wait much longer, Jesse. You better get it done."

Jesse's anger bloomed into something raw and hot. He walked swiftly past Flint, and swept the red pins off the map and onto the floor. Then he turned around and said, "I've got a hunch it's *you* who can't do the waiting, Flint."

Then he stormed past Hiram to the front door. Just before stepping outside, Jesse turned back and snarled, "But don't you plan on this being the end of it. Because there's more than money I got to settle with you now…"

Then he turned on his heel and slammed the door while Flint stared after him with fear.

Jesse walked toward The Pearly Gates and paused as he saw an unfamiliar piebald, heavily outfitted with gear, hitched to the rail in front of the "hotel." He climbed the porch stairs and stepped inside what was once a handsome, opulently furnished pleasure palace of the plains. It was now shabby and dark.

The front parlor was unoccupied, but he saw Pete standing behind his bar to the left of the front entrance. He also saw another man; tall and lean with a lined, savage face. He had one arm draped possessively across Trudy's shoulders. Jesse could see that his favorite prostitute, a good girl come to a bad place, was trying to be friendly to the man but only looked scared.

As he walked up to the bar, Jesse heard Pete stammer, "It sh…should be about ready, Mister Trey… just be a couple more minutes."

Jesse thought that old Pete, who wasn't afraid of much, looked almost as frightened as Trudy. Pete looked toward him, and said, "Be right with you, Jesse!" Then he moved quickly through the door leading into the kitchen.

Jesse gazed over at Conchita, who looked back at him with dark, lascivious eyes. He didn't mind the Mexican girl, but it always felt to him like she wanted to sink a knife into his back… in everyone's back—such was her anger at the world in general. Still, seeing that Trudy was indeed, engaged, he knew that beggars couldn't be choosers.

He lifted one finger at her and she nodded. He wanted a steak dinner and a couple of drinks before he submitted to her caresses, and Conchita knew it. She walked up to the bar, helped herself to a healthy shot of whiskey and sat down to wait with Owley.

He said, "Good evening, girls and Mr….?"

Trey turned at the neck to regard Jesse. He opened his mouth to say something, but Pete came out of the kitchen carrying an enormous, sizzling steak on a platter. The smell of the beef made Jesse's mouth water, and he started to order one for himself when Pete said, "Mister Flint says you was to have the very last steak in the house, Mr. Trey. So, here ya go…"

Pete looked apologetically at Bolt. They both knew how badly Jesse would have liked to have that steak dinner, but Jesse saw that the old man was almost shaking in his boots and abruptly lost his anger to pity.

Seeing the softening in Bolt's eyes, Pete gulped and said, "Beans are comin' right up, sir." Then, he backed up and disappeared into the kitchen.

Bob Trey reached out and gave the whiskey bottle in front of his platter a light shove. It slid down the bar to Jesse who stopped its progress with his big fist.

"While you're waiting." Trey said.

Jesse regarded the bottle for a moment and then slid it back. "Sorry, it ain't my brand."

Trey gave Jesse a slow, appraising look, shrugged and started sawing away at his steak.

A sudden, breathtaking rage filled Jesse's chest like poison, and he stood up. He looked at Conchita and snarled, "Come on, then. If I can't satisfy one appetite, I'll look after the other."

Conchita downed her drink quickly and stood up to join Jesse Bolt, while Trey grinned and slowly ate the rest of his steak.

Chapter Twenty

Kate studied Jack's reaction to her exuberant lies and said, "Better get that beef carved, Jack. Before all these menfolk lose their appetite to the punch bowl!"

Ducking his head, Jack finished cutting the beef and then, as if Kate's previous statements weren't bad enough, she announced, "Gather around everyone, load up your plates, and then wait for a minute while Jack says the Blessing…"

Suddenly, for the first time in years, Jack felt an almost overwhelming embarrassment. He had not been asked to say Grace since he was a child—since he'd lost his family and his farm, left home, gone to war and come back finally, to a life of the gun. He simply did not know what to say and stood awkwardly by the meat table, speechless.

Kate's friends and neighbors stood around him silently, except for a baby that cried softly, somewhere in the crowd. Jack cleared his throat, took off his hat and frantically tried to come up with some appropriate words.

LINELL JEPPSEN & JEB ROSEBROOK

Even Kate sensed, belatedly, that she might have made a tactical error in asking Jack to say a prayer, but Jewel, sensitive to the gunslinger's anxiety, whispered, "Just ask for rain, Jack."

A unanimous buzz of agreement rippled through the crowd and, like a wolf suddenly released from a trap, Jack smiled and said, "Let it rain, and let's eat. Amen!"

THEN HE PUT his hat back on, the crowd laughed and they all began lining up to fill their plates.

———

A FEW MILES away from where Kate, Jack, Henry and Jewel sat down to eat with their friends, the Bolt boys rode four abreast across the moonlit prairie. They were eyeballing a small sod hut in the near distance. U.S. thought it belonged to a young couple named, Burroughs...*Yeah*, he thought, *Jake and Tina Burroughs, was what Pa had said.*

That was the brothers' first target. They rode up loudly calling out, "Hey... anybody home? And, "Hello, the house!" But there was no answer, and the small hut stayed dark. The boys looked to each other and grinned. Then, climbing down off their mounts, all four walked into the front door and began destroying everything in sight.

There was precious little, really, just a young couple starting out, but they threw the kitchen table and its two chairs, a pretty, roll-top desk and their tick bed out into a pile in the front yard. What *was* left inside; foodstuffs, bedding, clothes and assorted sundries they ripped down, tore, smashed and shredded.

They *did* find about twenty pieces of silver in a velvet pouch, a Bible, and four elaborate silver teaspoons. Except for the Bible, which joined the furniture in the pile, U.S. pocketed all the silver. He had a vague notion of giving the silver spoons to Jewel on their wedding night, but knew, in his heart, that his father would either take the silver—the girl—or both, for himself.

The brothers did their work in less than ten minutes and right before riding on to the next ranch, they set a bonfire to the Burroughs meager possessions. Whooping and hollering with glee, and a job well-done, U.S. and his brothers gave no thought to the fact they had just rendered the Burroughs couple destitute.

They rode for about a mile and a half, and came upon the next small farm. Once again, riding up politely enough, they sat their horses and called out, "Hello! Anybody home?"

Hearing no response from the bigger and more elaborate house, they climbed down from their saddles and set to work. This house was better provisioned, although nothing to write home about. Still, good husbandry was going on here and U.S. consulted his little hand-written list.

He squinted at his pa's hand writing and read, **Luke and Belle Clayton** homestead. He nodded in satisfaction. For some reason Jesse seemed to really have it out for Luke Clayton—probably because he had been good friends with Charlie Swain, and was one of Kate's best 'homemade' whiskey customers.

Also, U.S. thought, Luke probably hadn't kissed his

pa's butt cheeks with enough exuberance in the past. Jesse was prideful, U.S. knew, and demanded respect from one and all whether he deserved it or not. Somewhere along the way, old Luke had disrespected the Bolt's and now his pa was out for blood. *Destroy it all!* Jesse had underlined the sentence twice, and U.S. smiled.

He set his brothers to looking for valuables before setting the whole house on fire. And, miracle of miracles, Cale found a whole case of whiskey under the kitchen wash basin. They pulled the whiskey out of the house and each one of them grabbed a bottle for their own and started downing the alcohol like it was water.

Troy ran back inside the house, found a strongbox and hauled it outside. U.S. took a hammer to the padlock (they had decided earlier to stow their guns and rifles for this part of the evenings work because they all knew how sound traveled through the night air on these low prairies), and found both paper and silver money, land deeds, a string of pearls, a gold ring and a will; penned out for their grown children.

Drunk now, and getting drunker by the minute, the brothers did a little jig and threw a firebrand into the front door and windows. Then they stuffed their saddlebags with their booty, watched for a minute to make sure the house was alight and then rode toward the next ranch.

———

AS THE BOLT brothers did their worst, the folks at Kate's party were setting to with gusto. Henry sat at a long table closest to the punchbowl, and addressed the people seated next to him. "All it is, gentlemen, is in the finding. But, I can assure you, water's there…"

One young man named Jake, who was seated at the end of the table paused on his steak and asked, "But, where?" His tone was so plaintive Jewel couldn't help but wince and give Henry's ankle a little kick under the table.

Henry jumped slightly, but was undeterred. "Ah," he said, "that's the next step, of course. Finding it… pass the bread, Jack, and the whiskey."

Jack was eating his dinner and trying to mind his own business, but he stopped to hand a plate of bread and the jug of whiskey to Henry. He immediately tucked into his meal again, but a young woman was leaning on his left shoulder provocatively, and saying, "… and they couldn't take it and moved back to Omaha. Say, you must know Omaha very well, don't you?"

Jack chewed the tough meat for a couple of seconds and said, "Well, only parts of it…"

Kate's shrill voice cut into their discussion. "Look at him! He's supposed to be serving my whiskey, not drinking it all!"

The guests laughed, and after a moment, Henry joined in and filled his glass to the brim. The woman sitting next to Jack used the interruption to scoot even closer to him —so close that any sudden move on Jack's part would have her sitting in his lap.

She continued, "You know, they were very active in the Methodist church… perhaps you've met them?"

Jack, not feeling very religious at the moment, scooted away from the woman as much as he could and replied, "Well, that's one side of town, all right. But, you see, well —drilling takes me traveling all around the country…"

Jewel, who had been watching Amanda Lowry's antics with narrowed eyes, said, "Yes, he's always on the move…"

Amanda looked at Jewel, then at Jack and moved away from her tentative flirtation as Jewel gazed at Jack with naked longing and Jack realized with a sudden, uneasy jolt that he wanted her, as well.

Chapter Twenty-One

AT 12:15 IN THE MORNING, JESSE AWOKE WITH A START. He'd been put through the paces by Conchita and then left the girl snoring drunkenly and went to his own bed in one of the hotel's remaining rooms.

He'd headed downstairs to grab a bite to eat first, and made do with some beans and hock. Old Pete was morose and silent as Jesse shoved the food down and finally, he made his way back upstairs for some shut-eye.

He'd been sleeping soundly enough when horrible dreams filled his mind... dreams filled with fire and death. Heart pounding loudly in the aftermath of his nightmares, Jesse poured a drink of water from the pitcher by his bed. He stared out the dirty window of his hotel room at a small, high moon sailing across the late-night sky and thought he heard a woman's scream.

He walked over to the wall by his bed and leaned close to listen, but heard nothing more. Then he realized that he'd heard those same cries in his dreams—the sound of a woman on fire and screaming in anguish.

Shaking his head at his own fanciful anxiety, Jesse took another drink of tepid water, got back into his bed and fell asleep.

———

WILMA LLOYD SWAM to consciousness knowing something wasn't quite right. Her nostrils stung and her eyes watered. What made things worse was she had taken a liberal dose of whiskey (or as she called it, medicinal water) to take the edge off her aching back.

Normally a spry 85-year-old who could work circles around her beloved, but lazy daughter-in law, Anne, Wilma had wrenched her back spading the tater patch out back and was temporarily out of commission and laid-up in her bed.

She had wanted to go to Kate Swain's party but couldn't face the ten-mile ride in the buckboard to get there, so she had stayed behind while Sonny and his wife kicked up their heels.

Now, as she tried to shake the whiskey fumes from her head and gasped out loud at the muscle spasms rippling across her lower back, Wilma hollered, "Sonny? Anne, is that you? Better check the woodstove… something's on fire!"

She stopped yelling though and started coughing uncontrollably, as smoke filled the upstairs rooms and flames licked the staircase. Not able to get up out of bed, and quickly overcome by the fumes filling her lungs, Wilma fell unconscious; only screaming once, loud and long as the fire touched her bedclothes and burned her earthly body to bone.

Right before setting fire to the Lloyd's house, which was a good ten miles or more from the Swain Cattle Company ranch, the Bolt brothers, intoxicated to the point of insanity, had reeled about the house and front yard; howling like wolves at the mean moon above, and shooting the farm animals, one by one.

The first to go was Spotty, a black and white cattle dog and the family pet. The next to meet its reward was their milk cow, Rosie. Then, Anne's flock of twelve Rhode Island Reds turned into moving targets. After the slaughter, Garland hauled a big leather-bound book out of the living room, and swaying in place read out loud;

'DEAR DIARY~ **March14 1876**

This is our third day of the rain and the river has jumped the banks for many miles around us. But we are thankful, for this assures us of a... bounta... Bounti...ful springtime this year. Signed, Granny Lloyd.'

TROY AND CALE staggered out the front door hauling a cast-iron bathtub by its clawed-feet. Screaming inarticulately, they took one-two-three swings and tossed the tub into the corral fence, knocking most of the posts and rails down in a clatter.

Had they not been deafened by their own inebriation, they might have heard Granny calling out in fear, but they simply started shooting their pistols at the tub. They yelled in delight at how most of the bullets ricocheted off the heavy iron and went every which a way; one round narrowly missing Troy's face.

Then, they set the place on fire. U.S. stood and stared as the flames whooshed up in a conflagration and said, "They don't build better fires in Hell, boys!"

Then they clambered onto their mounts and rode off into the night.

They would never know that Wilma Beaumont had been the belle of the ball at many a Southern cotillion. Or, that she had once been one of the 'Souths' great beauties with her bright green eyes and shiny black hair. That she had held her own during two Indian attacks with her long rifle as she and her young husband, Travis Lloyd, traveled west to start a new life in the Texas territory. That she had bourn four sons in her younger days and had lived to see only one of them grow to manhood.

She was the strength of Western expansion and the very heart that drove it, but as the Bolt brothers rode off into the night, they neither knew or would have cared that Wilma Lloyd was burning to ash in her own bed.

Chapter Twenty-Two

THE FOLKS GATHERED AT KATE'S PARTY HAD FINISHED eating and were now sprawled around the bonfire sipping coffee and the last of the whiskey punch. The mood was mellow and some of the smaller children were dropping off to sleep.

Suddenly, Kate's strident voice rose above the murmurs of the assembled guests. "Why, hell no. I'm not going anywhere! I'm staying right here, ain't you?"

There was a flurry of whispers as the adults perked up and listened. "Well?" she stared around at the shadowed faces. "…you *are* staying, ain't you? All of you?"

A masculine voice called out, "But you gotta admit, Kate, fifty cents an acre is a damn fair price!"

Enthusiastic agreement rippled through the crowd and a woman said, "It's more than fair—it's money. Something we haven't seen much of for a while!"

Laughter met the woman's words and Jack Ballard shook his head. *Kate's plan ain't working out so well*, he thought. *Doesn't she know by now that you can catch more flies with honey than with vinegar!*

Looking to his right, he saw Jewel step to his side. They shared a look between them—frustration at Kate's general belligerence, and dismay that their neighbors seemed uninterested in defending their own land, much less coming to Kate's aid in defending hers.

Jack saw Kate take a deep, shuddering breath, as though physically wrestling her sharp tongue into obedience. Then she said, "Fifty cents an acre! Mark me, this land will be worth twice that… just wait on the first drop of rain!"

"When it rains!" another woman exclaimed. "That's what Charlie Swain always talked about and what did it get him?"

The crowd stirred with disquiet as Kate searched their faces in defiant sorrow. The same woman added, "That was uncalled for, Kate. I apologize… I really do."

Kate seemed shaken and Jack stepped out of the shadows. "She weren't talking for Charlie Swain. She's speaking for herself." Turning toward Kate, he said, "Go on, Kate."

Kate pulled herself together and announced, "The Bolts—they tore up my fence line. How long before they tear up yours?" She studied the faces ringing the bonfire and growled, "Who do they think they are?

Her voice rose in passion. "We are the keepers of our land! We are wedded to it. At least I am and for me that means, 'Till death do us part'!"

Watching her mother speak and suddenly feeling the same possessive zeal, Jewel took Jack's hand in hers, and said, "Yes! 'Til death do us part!"

A man yelled, "Kate! Kate, we know how you feel. But, you can't blame us for having our doubts!"

Kate stared about at the buzz of agreement from her neighbors and yelled back. "Then collect your lousy fifty cents an acre! That's worth more than living off hope, ain't it?" Her cheeks had blushed a deep red.

Another man said, "Now, just hold on, Katie." It was her friend Luke Clayton. "Nobody here has sold out… nobody's moved—not yet, anyway."

Kate bent down and scooped up two handfuls of Texas dirt, allowing the soil to drift through her fingers. Turning to Luke and Belle she said, "Then do me a favor, Luke. Never forget the favors you and yours courted and curried from this soil!"

She stared into the night sky for a moment and continued, "I like to think there's more than me and Jesse Bolt that hold this land worth fighting for! Call me a fool —but you'd better know I'm enough of one to fill my soul with that kind of faith!"

She drew herself up tall and Jack saw her naked will to survive this drought; come hell or high water.

She said, "Don't you think I've shared your doubts? And, I know you shared mine the day we buried Charlie Swain. But, I'll tell you this. *NOBODY* can buy my life for fifty cents an acre!" she stopped and drank the last of the whiskey in her mug.

"If you should choose to stay, remember this. My name is Kate Swain. I am your neighbor. Lean on my strength and I'll be blind to my own weaknesses. Trust me for help and I'll be doing my best to never let you down. Not one of you!"

The crowd broke into spontaneous applause and Kate,

sensing at least some small victory in her speech, hollered, "Henry, more whiskey! Everyone's thirst needs attention. Especially mine!"

The tension in the crowd broke and laughter echoed under the cottonwoods.

Kate shouted, "Russel, Gertie... break out those fiddles! Grab your partner everybody!"

There was a general shuffle and some laughter as the folks got to their feet and the children awoke to the sound of music playing. Kate started clapping time and calling the square dance;

'Buffalo gals go round the outside,
Round the outside,
Round the outside
Bowing to their partners!'

HENRY CHANCE HAD STEPPED into the shadows while Kate made her speech, but he stepped into the firelight now. With a flourish, he bowed and held out his hand. "Our dance, sugar foot."

She smiled and danced with him into the firelit crowd.

Chapter Twenty-Three

By 12:30 ALL THE BEEF, CHICKEN AND SIDE DISHES HAD been eaten and the punch bowl was dry. After a good round of music and dancing, most of the neighbors had left for home, except for the bachelor brothers; Heck and Stewart Connors, who were sacked out in Kate's barn and dead to the world.

Henry had gone into the kitchen with Kate's permission and opened another bottle of her dwindling whiskey supply. Now the man and woman swayed together in the darkness as Henry hummed a waltz into Kate's ear.

He wanted very badly to kiss this ornery, proud woman of his dreams but Kate, watching his every move, was playing a coquettish game of duck and dodge. Henry tried to plant a kiss on her lips again and failed, but to his credit, he never missed a note of the waltz.

Kate grinned and watched her daughter and the hired gun stroll down toward the dried-up riverbed over Henry's shoulder. *Good,* she thought. *Maybe Jewel can seal the deal, if all my talk to the neighbors never did.* Because if there was one thing she knew for certain; there was no way that she and Henry could stand up to the Bolts alone.

———

JACK AND JEWEL walked along the sandy soil of the riverbed. Jewel, who had never partaken of her parent's whiskey, nevertheless felt emboldened, almost inebriated by Jack's presence.

She had decided, after taking Jack's rough hands in hers during Kate's speech that she was in love with the gun-slinger. Not so long ago, she would have discarded the notion; what on earth, besides trouble and heartache could come of a relationship with a man who used his guns to make living?

But she had changed her mind, or maybe it was Jack who had changed? When he stepped forward and urged the neighbors to listen to Kate and consider her heartfelt pleas for assistance, Jewel knew (or, at least, hoped) that Jack had decided to stay on and hitch his wagon to the Swain Cattle Company and its owners.

He was what she had always dreamed of in a man—handsome, strong and capable. So what, if he was a little too intimate with his guns? That kind of talent was a necessity these days, what with men like Hiram Flint and the Bolts dead set on taking from her and her mother land that wasn't theirs to take.

Jack walked with Jewel, and felt the girl's right breast press close to his left arm. He sighed with pleasure—and some measure of worry. He thought that the girl was infatuated with him, and it had been a long, long time since he'd felt a woman's embrace. Still, after this business between Kate and the Bolts was finished up, he planned on moving on.

He welcomed Jewel's affection—as a young and healthy man, but wanted to make sure she knew that he did not intend to stay on after their business was complete. He figured that she was a virgin and he didn't want to rob her of that valuable commodity… but she was not making it easy.

Jewel stopped suddenly, still firmly holding on to his arm and he spun around and stood pressed up against her from their upper bodies down to their boots. Then she lifted her face, stood up on her tiptoes and placed her lips on his.

Her kiss was everything built up from the first day she'd seen him in the dinner hall at school and since then… and Jewel gave her all to a man who had, until now, only been worshipped from a distance. And, Jack was damn-well impressed by her effort.

Just as he felt his manhood stir with desire, she broke away giggling. Then she walked over to the beach and sat down on the sand with a sigh. She sat upright -part tomboy and part beautiful young woman —and stared up at the moon for a moment. Then she said, "I'll tell you right out front, Jack. I'm in love with you."

Jack took an involuntary step backward. Then, thinking over the last couple of weeks and the extent of Kate's trickery, he stared at her with suspicion.

Correctly interpreting Jack's guarded expression, she shook her head. "And no. Nobody made up my mind for me… not my mother, or Henry. Just you."

Jack hesitated a moment and then walked over to join

her on the sandy bank. He stared straight ahead and said nothing until she finally said, "Jack?"

He looked down at her and said, "Some years... and an awful lot of miles between us."

Jewel smiled and took his hand in hers. Then she brought that hand to rest on her left breast, and murmured, "Feel my heart, Jack. It only beats for you..."

Then they were kissing. Softly, tentatively, at first and then passionately, as Jack's cautious thoughts were overwhelmed. Their tongues met, clashed and mingled together as one.

Jewel lay back on the sand and Jack bent over her ripe body. His hands roamed over her breasts and down, as she moaned with desire. So did he and then they were interrupted as the sound of hoofbeats filled the air and U.S.'s scream of thwarted love, jealousy and rage echoed down the dry creek bed.

Chapter Twenty-Four

THE BOLT BROTHERS RODE FOUR ABREAST OUT OF THE mesquite on the opposite side of the riverbed. Two of them, Troy and Cale, were ready with loops and U.S. was smack in the middle, riding directly at Jack and Jewel.

He gave no sign of stopping and Jewel screamed at his fast approach. Jack threw Jewel aside, out of reach of U.S.'s horse, but didn't have enough time to save himself. The horse rode right over the top of him as its rider shouted in glee.

Jack felt a hoof strike his ribcage and glance off the top of his head. He groaned and tried to get up and help Jewel, but Garland roped him from behind. He needed a second to catch his wind and stand up, but Jewel was also roped by Cale and jerked off her feet.

Jack snarled in rage as Jewel was dragged backwards and he started to struggle out of the lasso that held him but U.S. rode up close, took his boot from his tapadero stirrup, brought it back and used his heavy rowel to dig a ragged hole in Jack's chest. Jack doubled over in pain as blood welled up, staining his shirt red.

Jewel cried out, "Jack! Jack…!" But she was now tied fast to a cottonwood tree. U.S. turned to his brother, "Garland, get up to the house, fetch Kate and meet us at the potato patch."

Then he stared down at Jack and grinned as he saw the gunslinger's blood drenching the front of his shirt. "…and Garland?" he added, "have her bring along a plow. It's high time our hired man did some work around here, don't you think?"

The Bolt brothers sneered at their big brother's tone and to emphasize his point, U.S. drew his revolver and cocked the hammer back. Leveling the gun at Jack's head, he said, "Ain't that so, *hired man?*"

Jack glared at U.S. silently and U.S. said, "Or, maybe we should have Jewel's mamma pull your plow for you?"

Jewel called out, "U.S.! Put that gun away! Does Jesse know you're out here?"

U.S. frowned and answered, "I'm in charge here, Jewel." Then, looking at Jack again, he asked, "So, what's it gonna be, hired man?"

Ballard answered, "You can deal with me, boy, but leave Jewel and Kate out of this."

Incensed at being called a boy, U.S. waved his pistol in the air, and barked, "I'll deal with you, for sure, hired man. How 'bout me separating you from your brains?"

Jewel screamed in fright and Jack knew he was playing a high-stakes poker game now. He would have to play smarter than this angry young pup if he expected to get his revenge. Jack willed his heart to slow down, and replied, "You're giving the orders now, U.S."

The oldest of Jesse's sons stared at Jack for a moment, as if he had temporarily forgotten what this whole thing was about. Then he grinned. "Right, then let's get to work!"

Spurring his horse, U.S. knocked Jack down into the dirt again and then rode up close to where Jewel was tied to the tree. He jumped off his mount and cupped Jewel's chin in his hand.

She tried to jerk away from him, but he pinched her face hard and said, "I swear, hussy, before this night is over, I'll see to it you get to spark with a real man!"

As Jack lay in the dirt counting his injuries, and wondering how he was going to put a stop to this madness, Jewel wept in fear at the fury in U.S.'s eyes.

———

Garland rode ahead and caught Henry in his first successful kiss of the night. Kate had just allowed his lips to touch hers, when hoofbeats filled the air. She hollered as Henry was roped from behind and dragged over to the side of the house.

He yelled out in rage but was far too drunk to do much more than that—especially when he saw U.S. ride up out of the darkness, draw his pistol and point it at Kate's left temple. Even Kate was shocked into silence by this unexpected turn of events.

They stood still for a moment, bathed in the moonlight, when Troy and Cale appeared out of the shadows. The young men were slowly pulling Jewel and Jack behind their horses by ropes tied around their waists.

Kate saw that Jack was badly wounded. He was staggering in pain, but Jewel seemed unharmed and walked with her head held high. "What's going on here, U.S.?" Kate asked. "Have you boys lost your minds?"

U.S. glared at her in reply and said, "Troy, go inside and fetch some whiskey. I know Kate does a brisk business for the neighbors… she might as well be neighborly to us, too!"

Kate snapped, "U.S.! What's the meaning of this?"

U.S. stared her down and said, "Why, you went and hired on a new man, Kate. We just want to see how well he works, right boys?"

Cale and Garland nodded in agreement, and Cale said, "That's right, Kate. That's why we brung the plow."

"What…" Kate stared as Garland got down off his horse, grabbed one of her old plows and started lashing Jack into the traces. "Take that thing offa him, right now!"

She stamped her foot in anger but U.S.'s pistol kissed her temple again and he growled, "Take the reins, Kate. Do it now or I'll open fire, I swear it!"

Troy showed up with four bottles of her whiskey and the boys drank deep. Kate looked around at the Bolt brothers and saw that they were all as drunks as skunks, but she also saw that U.S. was dead serious. If she refused to pick up those reins, she knew that she, her daughter, Henry and Jack would all die.

She hadn't cried in years, not even after Charlie had put an end to himself, but she wiped an angry tear from her eye now and picked up the reins of her old plow. She said, "So sorry about this, Jack…"

Jack shrugged and started walking forward dragging the plow behind him. Kate called out, "Why on earth are you doing this, U.S.?"

Ignoring her question, U.S. said to Jack, "You and Kate is going to turn this tater patch, and if you go dropping on us, hired man, Kate is gonna have to carry your load. Savvy?"

Jack simply nodded, and put his back into pulling the plow, which was rough-going because the dirt was hard-packed and as dry as bone.

U.S., sensing the hesitation, brought his rope down, hard, on Jack's back. "Git!" he screamed as Jack bent over in agony.

The blood from his previous wound had begun to dry but sprang open again at his efforts. Kate tried to help by leaning hard on the plow but within seconds, her palms were cut and bleeding on the wooden handles.

Jewel and Henry cried out at the horror of what was happening, and Garland suddenly yelled, "Heeeya! Gityup, mule!" Then he brought a quirt down on Jack's head.

Jack saw stars then, and his knees went out from under him. He fainted dead away in the potato-studded dirt.

Chapter Twenty-Five

JACK AWOKE TO THE SOUND OF SCREAMS AND SHARP, nauseating pain. Blood ran down his face in a cool stream and he understood that Garland must have busted open the wound from the horse shoe that had glanced across his noggin earlier.

Garland was still standing over him, wheezing with excitement and looked ready to clobber him again if Jack didn't get up and pull the plow. The gunslinger rolled up on his knees, shuddered, and stood with the harness over his shoulders. Then he pulled again, and heard Kate say, "You boys are committing a crime here, ya know… if this man dies from his wounds, I'll head clear into Lubbock to find me a hangin' judge!"

Jack turned and started cutting in the third row and sure enough, tiny wizened potatoes started to pop from the soil. His eyes were glazed with pain, his shirt-front and back were wet with blood, and Kate realized that the man was only standing upright through his sheer will to survive.

Cale, standing close-by, screamed, "Move!" and lashed Jack's back with his rope. Jack saw stars again for a moment but came wide-awake at Jewel's scream. "No!" she shouted. "Keep your dirty paws to yourself!"

Jack looked over to the barn where U.S. was running his hands up and down Jewel's body while Henry snarled and tried to break free of his bindings. Then he heard U.S. say, "You're coming home with me. To finish up what you started with *him*!"

Jack started to shrug the plow reins off his back to help Jewel, but Garland knocked him down again.

Kate let go of the plow handle and shouted, "She ain't going home with you, U.S.! Not if I can help it… hey! Take your hands off her titties!" She ran toward U.S. with her hands held up in the air like claws.

U.S. stopped fondling Jewel, but grabbed the girl's hair and started to mount his horse. Seeing Kate approaching, U.S. hollered, "Don't be afraid, Troy! Go ahead and knock the old gal down!"

But it was too late. Kate ran right over the top of the youngest Bolt and tried to pull her daughter from U.S.'s grip. "I said," she howled. "let my daughter go!"

By now, Jewel was up on the horse with U.S. She was fighting him, and Kate was turning in a tight circle along with the panicked horse, trying to pull her daughter down, but both women were losing the fight.

Jack had finally succeeded in getting free of the harness, but his head was spinning so severely from the multiple blows he'd sustained, he took two steps forward to help Kate and fell flat on his face; to the delight of the Bolt boys, who hooted and hollered in glee.

U.S.'s horse-fed up with the crazy humans

surrounding it, reared backward and one of it's front hooves hit Kate in the thigh, knocking her down to the ground. By now, Troy was also on his horse and he kicked his mount so hard it almost trampled her.

Unafraid at the close call, Kate stared up at U.S. and pleaded, "Give her back, U.S., please!"

U.S. ignored her, and shouted, "Garland, Cale, let's go!" Then, he and his youngest brother Troy took off toward the Bolt Lightning ranch.

For a second, Jack thought that Garland and Cale would take off without molesting him further, but the last thing Garland did was bring the butt of his pistol down over Jacks already wounded skull.

Then he knew no more.

———

JACK WASN'T sure how long he was out but when he woke up, he saw that both Kate and Henry were gone. He could hear Kate's voice, though, urging Henry to, "Hurry up, dammit!" and the sound of hoofbeats receding into the distance.

He got up slowly, mentally assessing the damage to his body. He reached up and felt his own skull wincing at the tenderness, but didn't think he was concussed. His chest and back felt like they were on fire, but again, he knew he would survive those cuts and bruises. The most trouble-some injury was his broken rib… or ribs. He could hardly draw a breath without a deep, wracking pain around his heart and lungs.

He'd heard stories told of broken ribs actually deflating a man's lungs, or piercing his heart. Looking up at the house, he knew his ribs needed to be wrapped before he could go fetch Jewel back home.

Moving gingerly, Jack stepped up the porch steps, and entered the house. Kate and Henry were gone but two old men were cowering in the corner of the kitchen by the grandfather clock, which read: 3:21. They clutched at one another in fear as Jack, covered in blood from head to toe, walked inside. Jack frowned and barked, "Who are you?"

The old men stared at him and then at each other. Finally, one of them said, "Uh, we're neighbors; Kate's neighbors, Heck and Stewart Conners. We were sleepin' it off in the barn when we heard the ruckus. By the time we got to the house, Kate and Henry was gone!"

Looking at Jack's bloody face and shirt, Heck added, "Looks like you could use a hand, son. What can we do to help?"

Chapter Twenty-Six

Jack saw the grizzled old men staring down at him with concern and for a moment his heart broke. In his life so far, kindness and compassion had been hard to come by. He wasn't used to it and he was touched.

He nodded. "I could use some help with wrapping my ribs… one or two of them are broke, I'm sure. But, the main thing is—once I take off—I need someone to send a telegraph off to Sheriff Amos Brisbane in Lubbock."

He studied the men in front of him, and asked. "How much did you two see, or hear?"

Stewart answered, "Well, I seen it all, I reckon. Heck was still snoozin', but those Bolt boys had you trussed up in that old plow and made Katie drive you across the patch. I also seen 'em whup you and almost run Kate over. Both me and Heck saw what he was doing to little Jewelry, and we seen 'em ride off with her, too. It was a kidnapping, plain and simple!"

The old men were as ruffled up as Banty roosters and Jack couldn't help but grin at their indignation. He nodded at them and said, "Good, you saw enough. So, what I want you to do is head to the closest telegraph office and call for Sheriff Brisbane. He's a good man and a fair sheriff. Ask him to come here as soon as possible, okay? Tell him that Jack Ballard asked for his help."

Heck had filled a basin full of water and put two rags in it to clean Jack's wounds. He said, "We can do that. Closest telegraph is about forty-five miles away in Ropesville. It'll take us a coupla days to get there, though. Is that fast enough?"

Jack nodded. "That'll be fine. I just want someone with… authority to know the truth of things around here. I expect that by the time he gets here, things will be pretty much played out, anyway."

Heck said, 'Okay, we'll leave as soon as we get you sorted out." He frowned, adding, "Pull your shirt off, Jack, so we can see what's what…"

Jack grabbed a jug of whiskey, considered it for a moment, and then pulled the cork. Taking two long pulls, he sighed and pulled his shirt off. He winced as the cloth, which was stuck to his skin with dried blood, tore at the wounds and started new blood flowing down his chest.

Stewart tsked, and dabbed at the wounds with the tepid water. Heck poked around on Jack's head and murmured, "Well, you got yerself a nice goose egg, but I don't think it broke your skull bone any." He dabbed at the spot with a rag and asked. "You want me to bind it for you?"

Jack said, "No."

He couldn't be walking around with bandages on his head and body or looking infirm in any way. Not right now. He needed to come in on the Bolt's looking strong… invincible. Not like some sort of cripple.

"Think Katie will mind if I tear up one of her sheets?" Stewart asked.

Jack said, "If she does, I'll pay her for the trouble." He pointed down the hallway and said, "That's Jewel's room. Use one from her bed."

Stewart hustled down the hall and Jack said, "Heck, you and Stewart need to be careful the next few days. I don't know what's got into those Bolts, but they are out for blood and I don't think they are respecters of women or elders. I'd hate to see you or any of the neighbors getting hurt while you're waiting on the sheriff."

Heck took note of the fact that the young well-driller hadn't included himself in the equation but let it go. Instead, he said something that had been eating away at him for a while. "You know, what I think got into the Bolt's is Hiram Flint…"

Then Stewart was back in the kitchen, tearing one of Jewel's sheets into strips. The two men wrapped strips of cotton around Jack's ribs, while he hissed in pain and took one more swig of whiskey to steady himself.

Heck continued, "That Flint ain't no better'n a road agent what with his high interest rates, and dirty tricks. Me and Stewart was lucky—we ain't got no mortgage on account of our pappy bought the whole parcel free and clear over thirty years ago. But that didn't stop old Flint from trying to turn our pockets inside out for water and feed. We got plenty of feed set by and head into the next county for the water we need.

"But he done the same thing to a lot of folks around here who had nothing held back, and they'll never be free of their debt to him! We didn't take any of his hinky money, though. He got no satisfaction from us—no, sir!"

Finished with their wrap job, the old men stood back and watched as Jack turned and grabbed his pistol and gun belt off the wall by Charlie Swain's portrait.

The younger man looked out the window and saw that the horizon was starting to brighten with the coming dawn. True sunlight was a-ways off yet, but Jack knew he had to hurry if he was going to head Kate and Henry off from their head-long dash to the Bolt Lightning ranch.

Turning back to the old men, he smiled and said, "Thanks for your help, gents. Hurry up with that tele-graph so Sheriff Brisbane can hear the truth about what's going on here, and be careful. Don't go tangling with those Bolts, okay?"

The Conners ducked their heads and nodded as Jack Ballard stepped outside and headed towards the bunkhouse to grab some fresh clothes, his carbine and his horse. Anyone who looked at Jack's face at that moment would have known he was no well-driller.

————

A FEW MILES east of the Swain ranch, one after another of Kate's neighbors had found what was left of their homes. Two of the houses were merely burgled and vandalized. Some of the womenfolk cried at the loss, but most of them were tough prairie hens who knew that belongings could be replaced. Besides, most of their valuables had been sold or hocked already, because of the drought.

Two of the neighbors, though, were driven to their knees in shock and sorrow. Jake and Tina Burroughs saw that everything they owned was gone—even the twenty pieces of silver that had been given to them when they married. They were destitute now and would have to scrounge up enough money—somehow—to board a train and head back to Tina's parents home in Pennsylvania.

Luke and Belle Clayton suffered the most. Ash and soot had stung their noses for the last few miles when they turned down their own road toward home. Luke was not terribly shocked to see that his house had been set ablaze, but felt a pang of sorrow thinking about his mother. Belle had started weeping with fear immediately at the thought of what might have happened to Granny Lloyd, who was a task-master but beloved by everyone who knew her.

Once their worst fears were realized; Granny, their milk cow, their chickens and their dog all burnt to ash, Luke grabbed his rifle. A sensible man never traveled without a firearm in this country. There were too many coyotes, cougars, and wolves; not to mention the occasional renegade Injun in the region to go around unarmed.

Belle didn't know what Luke was going to do; he just set about his plans as usual, without consulting her about it. His mouth was downturned in a bitter grimace as he made sure his pistol, shotgun and two rifles were loaded, and ready for action.

Then, he walked up to where she stood staring down at the charred remains of their family Bible. Belle put her hand on his arm and murmured. "What you plannin' to do, husband?"

Luke shook his head and tears trickled down his cheeks. "Dunno," he answered.

Belle sighed. "For now, let's just grieve, okay?" She took his gnarled old hand in hers, and added, "After that, we'll head on back to Kate's place. Maybe ask that *"well-driller"* for help."

Luke had to smile. His Belle was no fool, and although they hadn't talked about it yet, he wasn't surprised to find that she had as many doubts as *he* did regarding Jack Ballard and his so-called, well-driller occupation.

He agreed with his wife. It might take some time for the house timbers to cool down enough to find Grannie's bones and lay her to rest. In the meantime, they could maybe butcher the cow for the meat, salvage some of Belle laying hens for the cook-pot and bury old Spotty in the family plot. He'd been a good dog and didn't deserve to have his carcass torn apart by coyotes as his reward.

They could put their place to rights, mourn his ma, and take stock of the situation. But then, after the grieving was done, he would go after whoever did this. If it was the last thing he ever did.

Chapter Twenty-Seven

THE SUN BROKE OVER THE HORIZON IN A HOT BRILLIANT display, and with it came a gust of blowing dust. Kate, who was in the middle of arguing with Henry, paused and coughed as airborne dirt flew into her mouth and down her throat.

She *had* been yelling, 'Strength in numbers! That's what you say, but Jewel is my daughter…" when she was overcome.

While Kate hacked and spit, Henry took the opportunity to say, "Katie—we still got time enough to gather up the neighbors!"

They were sitting on the wagon bench and stopped in the middle of the road leading toward the Bolt Lightning ranch. Kate was armed with her pistol and her Hawken Plains rifle, and Henry held the horse's reins. They were arguing about whether to approach the Bolts right now or wait for a while until they could gather up reinforcements.

· · ·

KATE GLARED AS HENRY CONTINUED, "That way we can outnumber them… out gun them! Those Bolts wouldn't chance odds like that!"

Kate reached over and grabbed the reins from Henry. She hissed, "Give me those…"

Henry surrendered the reins but insisted, "Kate! Shooting means killing! Killing means dying—maybe even Jewel!"

But Kate answered, "Nobody's asking you to be a part of this Henry! Because, right now, you're about as useless to me as tits on a boar hog!"

She faced forward and started to twitch the reins when she saw an apparition emerge from the rising dust. Ballard was approaching, looking exactly as he had on the first day he'd arrived. The same clothes, his long-barreled pistol, the carbine in its boot.

He stopped his horse and regarded the two people on the wagon. His eyes were dark and cold, and his mouth was a thin-lipped slash. Kate had never seen Jack like this before, and she was emboldened by his presence.

She said, "I was just telling Mr. Tail between his Legs here…"

Jack interrupted, "I heard." He moved his horse up to the wagon and stared Kate down. "We'll do it my way."

———

A COUPLE HOURS LATER, Jesse took a left at the crossroad leading from Flint's bank, casino and feed store. His wagon was loaded down with feed and barrels of water. He was served a tasty breakfast and had been serviced in other ways the night before, so his demeanor was calm and satisfied. He planned on going home, having the boys feed and water the livestock, and then head on over to talk to Kate—with a little back-up.

The "back-up" followed behind him about three quarters of a mile. Hiram Flint and Bob Trey were traveling in Flint's black buggy, with Trey's horse tied on the back. Hiram clutched the horse's reins nervously as Trey gazed straight ahead with reptilian eyes.

Flint had hired Trey to get rid of a gunslinger named Ballard who was in the employee of Kate Swain. Bob chewed the inside of his cheek with a nervous twitch he wasn't aware he had.

Jack Ballard. Why was that name so familiar to him? And, why did that name make his skin crawl? He frowned and tried to think. Did he know Ballard from the war? Was he an officer who had chased Trey down at some point during the conflict… or was Ballard the law?

Most gunfighters lived (or died) off their hard-earned reputations. Other men in the field studied up on their potential rivals with the zeal of a "Straight A" student. Every move they made; the guns they carried, their individual quirks and weaknesses were scrutinized down to the last detail. They quizzed their competition as though their lives depended on it, because it often did.

But, for the life of him, Trey could not recall Jack Ballard being in the gun-slinger business. So—a lawman? A man in his field also knew the local law and again, the name 'Ballard' did not ring any bells. Which meant that Ballard was an unknown element… a fact Trey did not appreciate at all.

A wall of blowing dust and dirt suddenly rose up off the ground enveloping their buggy and hiding Jesse Bolt from view. Looking around at the elements, Trey was tempted to call the exercise off—at least until visibility was better, but Flint was in an all-fire hurry to get things sorted as soon as possible.

In addition, Trey had taken his payment up front, and that payment was substantial… enough to set Trey up for life—if he was willing to settle for less rather than more. At any rate, the money was good, and Trey was loath to part ways with it.

He hunkered down and pulled his kerchief up over his mouth and nose, while Flint sneezed helplessly against the dust's onslaught.

Chapter Twenty-Eight

JESSE, FOLLOWED BY HIRAM FLINT AND BOB TREY HAD JUST started down the road from Flint's outfit when Kate and Henry pulled the wagon to a stop out of sight of the Bolt's main house. The wind was doing a good job of hiding their presence; kicking dust and tumbleweeds up from the ground, making the windmill squeak and shudder and slamming the barn door back and forth.

The watchtower stood empty, but for a Winchester carbine and the dusty telescope. The outhouse was right under the watchtower, and was currently occupied. The wind hummed around the verandah and moaned through cracks in the walls. It also covered the sound of Henry's footfalls as he jumped from the wagon and scampered toward the watchtower.

Looking over his shoulder at the outhouse, Henry climbed rapidly up the ladder. Kate was watching his progress with tense interest, impressed despite herself at the sixty-four-year old man's alacrity. Even Charlie, who had been as tough as rawhide in his prime, couldn't have made that run as quickly as Henry did and with such grace.

Henry made it to the top, popped through the access door and hid just in time… a muted grunt sounded from within the outhouse. A shadow at the back of the Bolt's house paused, momentarily, then continued on its way and disappeared.

Kate was sitting on the wagon bench, watching as Jack made his way around the back of the big house, and Henry sat in the watchtower looking down at the honey pot. They were set and ready to go…

———

"COME ON DOWNSTAIRS, Jewel. Breakfast is ready," Troy growled.

Jewel opened her eyes and gazed up at the younger man with loathing. She remembered feeling sorry for this kid, once. She had heard about Mrs. Bolt's passing as a little girl, and had grieved for the Bolt brothers' loss. Sometimes her own mother, Kate Swain, made Jewel mad or embarrassed her to death, but even as a young girl she knew that she would be lost without Kate's presence.

But her sympathy had died last night… along with her innocence and joy for life. Troy and his brothers had robbed her of everything she had to give. Jewel knew that the drought had been hard on folks—her folks too, but she would never have believed that these young men; her neighbors, contemporaries and childhood buddies, would take turns raping her. But she was wrong.

Tears welled up and leaked down her cheeks, as Troy

snapped, "You hear me, girl? U.S. wants you, so get up and come downstairs with me!"

Jewel sat up and put her feet on the floor. Her dress was torn down the middle, exposing her breasts and she pulled a grimy sheet off the bed and used it as a sort of shawl to hide what was left of her modesty. Standing up, she looked around the scene of her humiliation, U.S.'s bedroom.

The room was in a state of squalor… dirty dishes, soiled clothing and empty whiskey bottles littered the area and filled her nostrils with foulness. Wiping her tears away, Jewel stepped out into the hallway and saw a rooster perched in an open window. It was squatting on the sill with its head under one wing as wind and dust ruffled its feathers.

Next to the rooster, on a once elegant but now scratched and dusty side table sat a portrait of U.S. He was duded-up after a trail drive and sat in a chair with his legs crossed. He was wearing a suit but had those big Mexican rowels on his dusty boots. Jewel paused in front of the picture, screwed up her lips and spat on it before Troy could stop her.

Troy lifted his arm to strike her but hesitated, lowered his hand and blushed. He was hungover, and had a piercing headache. He was no hand at drinking whiskey like his older brothers were. He had only, ever, had a sip or two before one of his siblings, usually U.S., took the bottle away from him. That was why he had passed out for a couple of hours and woke up sick but fairly sober.

He grimaced in confusion, and thought, *Things got out of hand last night, but surely, I didn't take part in that rape… did I?* He honestly couldn't remember. It was as if a hungry rat made of anger and alcohol had burrowed away at his brain and eaten up a piece of last night's party.

Glancing down at Jewel Swain, Troy gulped. He had loved little Jewelry since he was a sprout, and wouldn't have dreamed of hurting her in any way. But from the way she was staring at him now he realized with a sinking heart that he must be just as guilty of rape as his brothers.

He took her arm gently, and said, "Come on, Jewel. We don't want to make U.S. mad, do we?"

Jewel Swain didn't answer him, but stared straight ahead with a woman's hurt, a woman's fierceness and a dazed passivity as she followed Troy down the stairs.

———

JEWEL SAT at the table and tried to keep from vomiting at the smell of breakfast and the sight of the Bolt brothers seated on the opposite side of the table, eating their eggs and bacon and grinning at her like the devil's own imps.

U.S. was missing, but Cale and Garland were gazing at her with lustful, prideful grins. Only Troy seemed subdued and stared down at his food with a pale face. She sighed and wished with all her might that she could just snap her fingers, and find herself in yesterday with her innocence and her joy of the world intact.

Instead, Cale shoved his half-eaten plate in front of her and grinned, showing that he had not chewed or swallowed his last bite of egg, as his tongue and lower teeth were slimy and yellow with yoke. He said, "Go on… eat. I'll share with you. I mean, you shared with me, so I'll share with you!"

Garland tipped his head back and roared with laughter. "Why, she likes to turn down just damn near every-thing offered to her, don't she?" he sneered.

Jewel turned abruptly to the side, so nauseous she was sure she would puke, when she heard her mother's voice call out, "JEWEL SWAIN!"

Although Troy had sobered up a bit, Cale and Garland were still as drunk as they'd ever been. They stood up and wavering unsteadily on their feet, whirled toward the voice coming from the front yard. They pulled their guns, staring out the front door and then heard a quiet voice behind them say, "Over here, boys."

Chapter Twenty-Nine

Jack had snuck in the back door and hidden behind a large, filthy cupboard in the kitchen. From where he stood, he had a clear line of sight into the dining room and he watched as the Bolt boys ate their breakfast and boasted over their deeds the night before.

Although the two young men—Cale and Garland—were still stinking drunk, Jack was appalled at how callous they acted as they bragged over the rape of Jewel Swain. He was tempted to end it for them right then and there, but before he could act on his impulse, footsteps sounded on the staircase.

He saw the youngest boy, Troy, leading Jewel down the steps and his heart sank. He had hoped, somehow, that the brothers were full of hot air and that the purported rape was some sort of drunken, thwarted fantasy. He'd prayed that reason would prevail over the brothers' actions last night but one look at Jewel's face told the tale.

Jack understood now, that once the boys had kidnapped the girl they'd done their worst. Her face was battered, her upper lip was bloody, and she wore some sort of dirty shawl over her dress, which was torn into shreds.

Worse, though, was the expression on Jewel's face. All the joy, hope, pride and strength of youth was stripped away, leaving only a shell of the young lady Jack had grown to appreciate and started to fall in love with. His heart ached for her loss, but his soul cried out in anger. Judging the trajectory of his bullets, he stepped out from the kitchen and said, "Over here, boys."

And his fury was pleased to see their reaction. Cale, Garland and Troy pulled their pistols and Jack, holding his Colt with one hand, worked the filed-down hammer of the gun with the other hand. The gun exploded three times in just under two seconds, before the boys were even able to open fire.

Cale disappeared, knocked off his feet and thrown clear through the partially open front door. Troy was hit in the chest and the bullet's concussion slammed him against the far wall. Garland was shot in the face and he flew through the front window taking broken glass with him.

Jewel had jumped up and run toward the kitchen. Now, with the sudden silence, she stopped and gazed down at the brothers in shock. Three of the boys who'd raped her were dead now and their killer stood over them with cold, deadly eyes. Part of her was glad, but she was filled with horror. She'd known these boys her whole life and now they were as gone as gone could ever be.

Her blood turned to ice and she looked up at Jack with a queasy mixture of adoration and fearful loathing.

Jack knew that look. . . he'd seen it before. On one

hand he was relieved. He'd never intended on staying and Jewel's rejection would save him time and her any hurt feelings. Still, he stepped over Troy's body and walked up to her.

Putting his left hand on her cheek, even as his right hand held the smoking Colt, Jack stared into the young woman's eyes. "You'll be okay now, Jewel," he said softly.

Nodding, she put her hand over his and whispered, "I know. Thank you, Jack."

He put his arms around her for a brief moment, and heard her gasp. "Watch out!" she cried.

Jack pushed her away and whirled around to see that Troy had lifted his pistol and was taking aim at his back. The boy was mortally wounded, though, and Jack could see that his gun was aiming high and would miss him by ten or fifteen feet.

Troy said, "You… you killed us all!"

Then Jewel cried out at two new explosions. Both Troy and Ballard had shot, but Jack's bullet was the deadly one. Troy, shot in the throat, died instantly and Jack holstered his pistol.

Jewel was weeping by now, and Jack said, "I want you to stay inside while I take care of U.S., okay? Go upstairs and hide."

"But my mother…" she said.

Jack shook his head. "She's just fine. I can see her sitting in the wagon. You just stay here until I call for you." With those words, he stepped outside to finish his work.

———

JACK STOOD LOOKING DOWN at the ruination of Cale and Garland. Their bodies lay twisted and bloody on the front porch and both men still held their pistols. Jack kicked the guns away, and started walking toward the outhouse.

U.S. had heard the gunfire and knew that, even drunk, his brothers would not be firing on each other, so he figured someone was gunning for them. Now, hearing the sudden silence, he thought he'd better skedaddle or he might be the recipient of the next bullet. The wind was howling, which he knew would mask his moves, so buttoning his pants with one hand and clutching his pistol with the other, he slowly opened the rickety door.

The first thing he saw was Kate sitting in her wagon. Her mouth and eyes were wide open in shock. Feeling rage strike his gut, he lifted his gun to shoot her down when a huge knife thunked into the door a scant inch from his nose.

Henry was perched like a monkey halfway down the ladder and had seen U.S. take aim at Kate. He'd let his Arkansas toothpick fly and couldn't help but grin. Those knife skills he'd learned from an old gambler on the Mississippi River so long ago were still keen, it seemed.

Kate was not smiling, however, and lifting her Hawken, she pulled the trigger. Henry yelped and flew back up the ladder.

U.S. was kneeling by the smelly hole in the outhouse's bench when the whole top of the honey pot blew into splinters. Showered with what remained of the small building, U.S. threw his pistol to the ground, and climbed out of the rubble with his hands in the air. "I surrender! Don't shoot me, Kate. I surrender!"

About that time Jack walked up and bending over,

delivered an uppercut to the younger man's face. U.S. was hit so hard that he was catapulted five feet away toward the horse trough. Not finished yet, Ballard lifted the young man, who had been knocked cold, by the back of his collar and dragged him over to the closest tree.

Jack let U.S. drop to the ground while he casually slung his rope over a low branch and fashioned a noose. Then he proceeded to fasten the noose around U.S.'s neck.

Kate had been sitting in a state of paralysis. Although she had hired Jack Ballard for his fighting skills, seeing the result was almost more than she could bear. Three of the Bolt boys were dead by Jack's hand and now he was fixin' to hang the fourth!

"Jack!" she screamed. "Stop it, now. There's been enough killing for one day!"

Jack ignored her and started to heave U.S. up in the air by the rope around his throat, but Henry walked up to him. Kate held her breath... there was a wildness in the gunslinger's eyes that she'd never seen before and she was afraid for Henry's life.

The little 'water witch' stood steady, though, and put a hand on Jack's shoulder. Kate couldn't hear what Henry was saying but suddenly Jack stopped pulling on his rope and shook his head, as if he'd just woken from a deep slumber.

At the same time, Jewel ran down the porch steps from the house. "Mamma!" she cried. "Oh, mamma..." and then Kate's daughter was in her arms. The two women stood together, crying softly and taking comfort from each other's embrace.

Time stood still for a moment and then Jack threw U.S. down at Kate's feet. "You decide, then," he said.

Kate moved away from her daughter, walked to her wagon, removed a shovel and walked back to where U.S. sat on the ground blinking up at her.

She planted her shovel in the hard-packed soil and said, "Better get busy, boy. You've got some digging to do." Then, she looked past him toward the front of the house and U.S. followed her gaze.

Suddenly, as if the whiskey in his bloodstream had dissipated all at once, his eyes took in his brother's dead bodies and tears rolled, unchecked, down his face.

Chapter Thirty

U.S. SUDDENLY FELT HIMSELF PLUCKED FROM THE GROUND by his collar. Ballard had ahold of him again, and the younger man began cartwheeling his feet in the air. "No! Kate... he's gonna kill me, just like he done my brothers! Kate, stop him, please!"

Kate stood still and watched as Jack dumped U.S. on the ground, pointed at the dirt, and said, "Start diggin'."

Weeping, U.S. took the shovel and drove the blade into the rocky soil. Jack watched him dig for a minute or two and then walked over to the wagon, where Kate, Jewel and Henry were climbing aboard. Jack stepped up on his buckskin, who was skittish from the blowing wind, dust and sporadic gunfire.

His eyes and voice softened as he murmured, "Whoa there, Reb. That's a good boy..."

Jewel shook her head. Jack Ballard had shown no mercy to the Bolt boys and had dispatched them with hard, cruel efficiency, but he seemed to be a different man with his horse... gentle and kind.

Her mother's voice interrupted her musing, "U.S., where's your pa?"

U.S. looked up and whined, "He didn't have nothing to do with this! I swear..." Staring wide-eyed at Jack, he added, "Don't let him kill Pa! Don't let him do it!"

Kate, overcome with rage again, hollered, "You raped my girl... took her flesh!"

U.S., trembling in his own sweat, looked to Ballard who was reloading his Colt. Then Kate hissed, "U.S., if we ever cross trails again, ever again, I'm going to cut you off between the legs and let you bleed out for the buzzards."

Looking sick, U.S. started shoveling dirt again and Henry snapped the reins over the horse's backs. The wagon took off with Jack following behind.

———

THERE HAD BEEN AN UNSPOKEN RULE—OF late—not to cross over Bolt land, but Kate paid that no heed this morning. She just wanted to get back to the Swain ranch as quickly as possible, put her Jewel in a long, hot bath with lots of soap and swig enough whiskey to erase the sight of the Bolt brother's deaths from her mind's eye.

Henry seemed to feel the same, as he had not hesitated at the fork in the road but took the shortcut toward home. Suddenly Kate, sounding wretched, said, "Hold up a minute, Henry..."

He pulled back on the reins and watched as Kate leaned to the side and threw up. Henry felt like doing the same, but he simply patted Jewel's knee, and muttered, "Your ma's upset, honey."

Jewel touched Kate's shoulder as she heaved her guts

out, and Kate moaned, "Look at me, retchin' like a dog... I should be taking care of you!"

Jewel said, "You are."

Jack had been watching Kate, but a movement caught his eye and he stared ahead through the blowing dust. The first thing to appear was a pair of horses, and then Jesse emerged from the cloud perched on his wagon. The back of the wagon was filled with water barrels and sacks of grain.

Jack heard more noise and saw Flint's black horse and buggy pull up behind Jesse's wagon. Jack had no interest in Jesse Bolt, except for what he might do once he discovered his dead sons. He didn't care about the crooked little banker either—hell, shake a tree in West Texas and a crooked banker would fall out. But as his eyes met those of the passenger sitting next to Hiram, his heart started to beat slower... and louder.

This sort of thing had started happening to Jack back in his late teens, and had only grown more intense as the years passed. Moments of extreme danger and high stress brought it on, and often Jack thought of it as his own personal death knell.

Trey was feeling something similar, although his senses of danger came in the form of a high-pitched whining in his ears; like a mosquito smelling his blood on a warm, summer evening.

The two gunslingers studied one another for a moment, and Flint said, "Jack Ballard... meet Bob Trey." Hiram had a smirk on his face as though he'd just pulled an extra ace from a dead deck, but he'd clearly not seen the cold sweat that popped on Trey's forehead.

"We've met," Jack said.

173

Trey frowned and frantically tried to remember when he'd run across this man, but his thoughts were interrupted as Jesse addressed Kate. "What is it you want on my land, Kate?"

Kate's face turned red and she swallowed. "I'm… I'm sorry, Jesse."

Jesse saw the look in her eyes and heard the tone in her voice and for a moment, he felt a strange kinship between one tough, long-standing neighbor to another. But then he snapped, "What're you apologizing for?"

Then, looking Ballard up and down, Jesse said, 'You been at my place? By the looks of *him*, I'd say he could've been picking fights with my boys, again!"

Ballard turned sideways on his horse, and said, "Henry, get this wagon out of here."

Suddenly, Trey got out of the buggy, uncoiling his long body to stand at full height. Staring at Ballard with lizard eyes, he fingered his sidearm and let a grin pull at his lips.

Jesse, feeling a shudder of fear go up and down his backbone demanded, "Kate! Tell me what the devil's going on here!"

Trey took a step forward, but Jack looked right through him.

Kate, flushing, yelled, "Since you're the devil's partner, why don't you ask him?" She pointed at Hiram Flint. "Ask him what he's doing with that floor flushing gun-toter!"

Flint shook his tiny fist and hollered back, "You started it! Hiring him! Jack Ballard…now, Jesse's even with you."

Jesse turned abruptly, and stared at Bob Trey with appraising eyes. "Trey, get back in the buggy, dammit! We're leaving…"

"Henry, go on now," Jack said, and Kate's wagon lurched ahead, barely missing Flint's black high-stepper.

Trey stepped back inside Flint's buggy and it took off, following Jesse, who stared at Jack with worried eyes as he passed by.

Trey tipped his hat at Jack, but quailed at the expression in Ballard's eyes.

Jack sat and waited until the wagon and buggy were out of sight and then he turned his horse and galloped after Kate's wagon.

Chapter Thirty-One

Jesse's ham-like fist slammed into his son's face and U.S. flew backward, nearly into a partially dug grave. Jesse was screaming, "You went ahead and did it… went against my wishes! Disobeyed me and got my sons killed!"

Then, he roared inarticulately and fell on U.S. again, punching him repeatedly across the ground in a frenzy of grief and rage.

He glanced a blow on the young man's ear and grunted, "I ought to make you dig your own grave!"

Then, he stopped and bent over, hands on his knees, heaving. U.S. was bawling like a baby and ready to jump up and flee if it looked like his father was about to start hitting him again. Jesse studied the bodies of his three, dead sons laid out in a row with their hands and arms folded across their chests.

Furious again, Jesse grabbed the back of U.S.'s collar and the younger man cried out, "Pa! I'll make it up to you… I swear!"

Jesse threw him down in disgust and U.S. wailed, "Let me kill him. Me! I'll kill him dead, you'll see..."

Bob Trey, standing to the side and watching the show snickered at U.S.'s bravado, but Flint frowned and told Trey to shush. Stepping forward, Flint said, "Jesse, taking it out on him isn't going to solve your problem."

Jesse looked up and some of the starch went out of him. Staring at Hiram, he saw the little banker point at Trey and say, "But, he can. . ."

Jesse studied Trey's tall, lanky frame and mumbled, "Only if I can't do the job myself."

U.S., having gotten to his feet and wiped blood from his nose and mouth, stepped toward his father and said, "Only if *we* can't do the job, Pa."

Jesse took U.S. down with a withering glare and snarled, "Start digging."

———

KATE, Jewel and Henry were approaching the Swain ranch at a good clip and, as usual, Kate and Henry were arguing.

"Henry, I told you once, you can go or stay. Suit yourself!"

Henry shook his head and gave the reins a frustrated twitch. "Then you better face up to it, Kate. The killing has just begun!"

They pulled into the ranch proper and the dogs started barking. Henry pulled the wagon to a stop under the cottonwood trees and said, "Only, the next graves may be our own!"

Kate, staring straight ahead, muttered, "I ain't backing off from what I never started!"

Henry answered, "Well, who's going to finish it?"

Jack rode up and helped Jewel down off the wagon. He winced with pain from his quick gallop and stepping off his horse but took a deep breath and said, "I will. I'll finish it."

He had been lagging behind the wagon a little, letting Kate and Jewel catch their wind, and giving himself a chance to plan for what he knew was coming. Also, he was trying to cope with the fact that the notorious outlaw turned hired assassin, Bob Trey, was now in the mix.

He'd lied about having met Trey, but he had heard about the man many years earlier, both from his time in the Army and later, from sheriffs' blotters all throughout the tri-state area. Bob Trey had spent most of his younger years with different outlaw gangs; robbing banks, trains and stage coaches. In that occupation, he was no better or worse than the usual scum.

But, what made Trey noteworthy was his brutality with women. He was notorious for his savage treatment of Negro and Indian women, and had been known to rape and torture them for days on end. He was kicked out of the Confederate army for his behavior and later, he'd been asked to leave—at the end of a gun—most of the gangs he'd ever signed up with.

Jack hadn't thought about Trey for years, and honestly thought the man had long ago come to a bad, but fitting, end. Still, here he was, and Jack knew that if he didn't win this contest both Kate and Jewel would suffer the consequences of his failure. Too bad the man was as good with a gun as *he* was.

He sighed and looked down at Jewel's face. The girl was pale and great bruised circles ringed her eyes. She waited for Kate to climb down, as if she had no steam of her own to walk inside her home. Seeing Jewel's distress, Kate hopped to the ground and took her daughter's arm.

She gave Jewel a small squeeze and said, "Let's get you into the house."

But, Jewel said, "I want to talk to Jack."

Henry clicked his tongue and moved toward the barn to start unhitching the horses from the traces.

Kate hesitated a moment, then walked toward the house through her scurrying chickens. She stepped up onto the porch, then turned around and waited for her daughter.

Jewel looked up at Jack silently. He didn't know what to do, or say. Finally, he murmured, "I didn't get there in time to do you no good."

She looked down at Jack's pistol and then reached out and pulled the .44-40 Colt from his holster. She frowned and ran her fingers over the deadly, hammer-filed weapon.

Henry was standing close-by and he heard Jewel ask, "If they hadn't taken me... would you have still killed them?"

Hesitating, Jack retrieved his gun and holstered it. He knew what she wanted... she wanted to hear that Jack loved her desperately and that was why he had been so brutal at the Bolt Lightning ranch, but that wasn't the truth of it. Sighing, he answered, "Yes."

Her avid gaze fell, as he knew it would, and Jewel walked away to join her mother. The two women entered the house and Jack walked over to his horse where he pulled his carbine from the saddle-scabbard.

Henry walked by him, leading the two horses to the pasture and said, "Only a kid with wet ears would ask a question like that."

Ballard shrugged slightly, acknowledging Henry's comment, but not particularly happy with it.

Chapter Thirty-Two

By now, U.S. had finished two graves and was starting in on the third. His arms were shaking with fatigue and his whole body was drenched in sweat. Hiram Flint and Bob Trey were sitting on the verandah, only a few feet away from where the brothers' blood had spilled on the floor boards. The blood and body fluids had dried and were covered with a film of dust.

They were watching U.S. work, and keeping an eye on Jesse, who was sitting by himself up in the watchtower. Bolt was sitting in front of his over-turned telescope but staring out at the dazzling sun, eyes glazed and mouth moving silently with his own internal dialogue.

Finally, he found his voice and murmured, "I loved my woman... I did. And, those sons we bred and brought into the world." His expression was bleak as he got to his feet and stood, staring out at the far horizon.

"My land," he continued. "my woman, my sons... we all prospered. Through Commanche wars, and droughts and blizzards. There were blessings mixed in with the bad."

Then, as if losing all his strength, he sank down on the small chair and hunched over—staring at his big hands.

"I went on after Sarah died. She gave up her last breath giving me my last son. I took her back home to her own country—Tennessee, and buried her there... among gentler people. Then, I came back home with no tombstone to weigh heavy on my heart... Nossir!"

He looked up with a half-smile on his face. He had the look of a man who was savoring a glimmer of hope—a dream. "I always did have the idea of finding me a new, ripe young woman again. Just got busy and kept putting it off. But, it's not too late." He grinned. "A capable man like me? Why not? I could sire a whole new crop of pups!"

Jesse stared into the sun and his Ahab eyes burned with anger. His hands seized the telescope and he hurled it over the side, watching it sail to the ground. He was hoping for some sort of spectacular destruction, but the scope simply bounced on the ground with a slight puff of dust.

He snarled in disgust. "Signs! Hope... damn them both! I look to the moon and it shows me not a clue to rain! I smell the wind and my nostrils fill with dust! I listen for the single howl of a coyote past sunrise and never hear a one!"

He stopped talking and heard nothing but silence—even the shovel had stopped its rhythmic dirge. Staring down at the unbroken telescope, tears finally leaked from his eyes.

————

BOB TREY WAS LOADING and checking his second gun; a

long-barreled pistol while Hiram paced restlessly across the porch. Flint was impatient, needing to know—to plan. Time was money—after all.

U.S. bent down and lifted Garland up in his arms. He considered asking either Flint or Trey for some help but one look at their cruel faces told him no help would be forthcoming. So, he half fell-half slid into the oblong hole clutching his dead brother to his chest.

Then, they all heard Jesse holler, "U.S.!"

Hiram stopped pacing and looked expectantly toward the watchtower, as Trey grinned.

Jesse, yelled, "U.S.! Answer me!"

U.S. had laid Garland out in his grave and stood up now, wincing at a sudden sharp pain in his lower back. "Yes, Pa. I'm here…"

Jesse climbed down the ladder to the ground. His face was resolute, and he said, "Saddle my horse and load my shotgun!"

Trey spun the cylinder of his long-barreled pistol and glanced at Flint who nodded with a small smile of satisfaction.

———

JACK SAT in Kate's kitchen and loaded his handsome Winchester carbine carefully, one cartridge at a time.

Kate sat across from him, studying Jack's profile intently, trying to reconcile his good-looking features with the cold-blooded killer who had just laid to rest three young men so quickly and with such efficiency.

Sitting before her on the table rested her 1860 Model Colt. It too had been cleaned and loaded. Henry was spinning an empty jug of whiskey, looking like he wished it was full to the brim. He said, "They'll be here soon enough… if they want the sun at their back."

Neither Jack or Kate answered him, and he sighed.

Kate got up and walked toward the front door. She saw the roasting sun resting on the horizon and her dogs sprawled around under the cottonwood trees. She said, "Good Jesus in heaven—how I wish it had rained yesterday…"

Jack looked up from his carbine and said, "So do I."

Jewel, lying on her bed in her bedroom heard the fervor in his voice and tears leaked from her eyes.

Jack went on to say, "As soon as I'm finished up here, I'll be on my way."

Kate nodded. "Well, I suppose there's always work somewhere… for men like you."

Jack gave Kate a cold look, but she ignored him and continued, "I can't say you leave us any better than you found us. No rain, the heat driving people insane. We're doomed for all I know. Doomed, or cursed—whichever you please."

Jack finished loading his rifle and levered the carbine closed. Then he said, "You'll stick it out, Kate."

Kate looked thoughtful, then pleased. She nodded and replied, "I will, won't I?"

Jack looked at the gun in his hands and said, "I've done my part . . . or at least I aim to soon."

Then, as if to punctuate his words, the dogs began to growl, and then bark.

Chapter Thirty-Three

JACK HEARD HOOFBEATS, AND THEN JESSE BOLT CALLED out, "Ballard!"

Jack turned away from Kate and looked out at the fading sunlight. The riders were not in the front yard, but hidden behind the trees or in the thicket ringing the back pasture.

Jesse hollered again, "I'm waiting on you, Ballard!"

Jack's eyes focused on something unusual and he saw Hiram Flint's buggy with Bob Trey's horse tied on the back. It was parked on the ridgeline above the dry river bed. He saw no trace of Trey, however, which meant the gunslinger was on the prowl—thus a wild card in this deadly hand.

Jack stepped back from the window, murmuring, "Yup, right on time."

Kate picked up her gun and said, "I'm going with you."

Jack stared her down and shook his head, but stubborn as usual, she cocked her Colt and started for the front door.

As quick as a wink, Henry rushed forward and plucked the gun out of her grip. "I'll take that."

Kate started to object but Jack shook his head at Henry too. "You ain't goin' along, either. Follow me out that door and I'll kill you."

Henry stared up at Jack and then he smiled; that irascible, wrinkled, cunning and polite grin that made Jack believe Henry would do okay by Kate and her daughter (if he stayed alive).

Again, Jesse's voice rang out. "Come out alone, Ballard. I'll settle with Kate later!"

Henry said, "Jack… I am but depriving the widow Swain from, in any way, being foolish enough to risk her life helping you."

Kate, impotent but still filled with rage, said, "And to think. They could have killed you last night!"

Jack shrugged. "Reckon I was worth the hurting, but not the killing."

He turned and headed for the front door. At that moment, Jewel ran from her bedroom, her eyes only for Jack.

From outside, Jesse screamed, "Ballard, I'm running out of patience!"

Jack stared briefly into Jewel's eyes, trying in his way to let her know that he did care; that he thought she was beautiful and worth saving, but he found no words to express his feelings and simply walked out the front door.

Kate, seeing the silent exchange, seized the opportunity to lunge for her Colt, but Henry was far stronger than he looked. "Give it to me!" she grunted, arm wrestling the wiry little man.

But he said, "No!" and shoved her backward.

Kate stepped forward again and hissed, "Give me my gun, you little turd!"

But Henry just smiled and answered, "Not on your life!"

Suddenly, Kate; the ornery, proud, tough as nails owner of the Swain Cattle Company, hunched over, covered her face with her hands and wept. "Rape! Murder, Madness... Oh Henry, it's madness!"

Henry stepped forward and put his arms around her. He patted her back while she bawled, and murmured words of comfort in her ear. Then, she stiffened when she heard Jesse holler, "When I finish with Ballard, I'm moving you out! Hear me, Kate?"

Kate sobbed against Henry's chest and whispered, "Henry... I never wanted to see my Charlie dead!"

Henry nodded. "I know, honey. He was a good man, and since he checked out you've needed a man around here, Katie. Of course, you do! Maybe now you'll know you have one—me!"

From outside, Henry, Kate and Jewel heard a carbine open up.

———

Jack paused and ducked down by the corral, then he made a run for the cornfield. Bullets were humming around him and he returned fire from his hip.

He dove for the cornfield and heard, "Whoom!"

That was followed by another shotgun explosion. Stalks, dry papery leaves and corn kernels swirled around Jack like shrapnel and he fell to the ground. He could feel a half a dozen tiny pinpricks where the demolished corn had snipped away at his flesh, and blood trickled down his face.

On his belly, Jack measured the distance to the thicket. He figured it was a twenty-yard run and, for now, the shooting had stopped. He got up and zig-zagged his way into the brambles, firing his pistol, but there was no return fire.

He dove under a large mesquite and belly-crawled toward the tree line. A second later, he heard another loud, "Shoom!" and the mesquite bush he'd hidden under a few moments before exploded into chaff.

Someone—probably Trey—had a bead on him. Jack knew he had to move, and quickly, or he'd be mowed down. He changed direction slightly, and slithered like a snake for better cover. He heard two blasts—"Whoom! Whoom!" But now, the shrubbery behind him was demolished.

———

JESSE PAUSED to reload his .10—gauge shotgun as U.S., more birddog than hunter, prowled through the brush.

Bob Trey waited patiently for Ballard to come to him, and Flint was watching the progress from the safety of his buggy. He was not so patient as Trey and was scanning the brush with his binoculars and a nervous scowl.

Ballard was pressed flat to the ground, and he could hear the sound of breaking brush. Then, lifting his head slightly, Jack saw Jesse directly in front of him. He loomed in the thicket like a great grizzly bear.

Jack knew he couldn't get behind Jesse, but he moved

enough to put the setting sun at his back. Then he said, "Tell 'em to toss their guns, or you're a dead man."

Jesse turned and saw Ballard and his Winchester carbine pointed at him. He fixed his eyes on Jack but refused to give up his shotgun.

Ballard said, "You're out of time…"

U.S. had snuck up as quietly as possible and now took aim at the back of Jack's head. But in that split second a twig snapped, and Jack dropped flat, rolling and firing at the same time.

U.S.'s bullet, intended for Jack, hit Jesse Bolt right between the eyes.

U.S., stunned, gasped, "Pa? Oh, Pa, no!"

But then he keeled over—both from the two shots Jack had fired into his body, and the fact that Jesse's reflexes had triggered both barrels of the shotgun in his hands, blowing most of U.S.'s body off at the shoulders.

Both father and son lay dead and bleeding out on the ground where Jack lay.

At that moment, Bob Trey stepped out of the brush and smiled. He did not have his guns out, but held his palms just above his holsters.

Seeing what was happening below him, Hiram Flint dropped his binocs and yelled, "Kill him where he lays, Trey. Kill him now!"

Jack glanced up at Flint, but Trey ignored the man who hired him and continued to grin down at Jack.

"Forget the reputation, Trey! Kill him now!" Flint howled.

Jack slowly stood up, watching Trey's every move, and said, "He right, you know."

Trey answered, "Oh, is he?" The gunslinger spread his

legs for balance, and held his hands mere inches from his guns. "Ever heard of me, Ballard?"

Jack understood then; to a man like Bob Trey, his power to generate fear and his confidence in killing was more important than life. To deflate that vanity a bit, Jack took two slow steps back, so now he and Trey were ten feet apart.

He lied, and said, "Nope, but I'm just a well-driller, Bob."

Bob frowned but said, "Well, I shoot that kind down just for practice."

Jack shrugged. "You don't say?"

Trey, getting angrier by the minute, snarled, "Them ain't much for last words…"

And Ballard reacted as the gunslinger went for his right-hand gun. Jack was a split second faster than Trey and the gun-toter took Jack's first slug in the guts.

Jack was creased on the shoulder and spun about. But, maintaining his balance, he turned and fanned his Colt. Twin explosions from the weapon tore and shattered Trey's body.

Bob lifted his head, glaring and tried to pull his left-hand gun but laid his head back and died instead.

Chapter Thirty-Four

Five days later Jack and Jewel rode toward the school. Both were quiet as they mulled over the events of the last week. Jack's face was bleak with pain, and Jewel could barely keep her sorrow and disappointment in check. Still, they rode on—resolute.

For two days after the gunfight, Jack had laid in his bunk, wracked with pain and fever from the gunshot to his shoulder, his broken ribs and the blow to his head. He slept, mainly, and only allowed Henry in the bunkhouse to help. Jack was occasionally prone to black moods and, at that time, the darkest of emotions filled his heart.

Three days after the shootings, though, Jack got up and accompanied Jewel, Kate and Henry to the Clayton's ranch for Granny Lloyd's funeral. Luke and his wife had found Wilma's burnt bones and were burying her that day, along with the family dog, Spotty.

All the neighbors knew about the Bolt's and it was agreed that the menfolk would ride back to the Swain ranch to help bury the bodies, after the funeral. There was no pastor in the area, so Luke made do with reading a few passages from their charred Bible.

There was no pot-luck after the service, either. No one had food or liquor to spare for such an indulgence. Hugs, and promises to help in any way they could were exchanged though and after about an hour they headed back home, with two men riding in the wagon, and a few more riding their horses back to Kate's to help bury the masters of their misery—Jesse Bolt and his sons.

While the men dug three graves—one for Jesse, one for U.S. and one for Bob Trey, Jack wished they were digging one more—for Hiram Flint. He knew that Flint was the architect of all this death, but he'd seen the little man drive away in his fancy black buggy once Trey had gone down.

Still… Jack gave a slight smile. Heck and Stuart Conners knew the whole story and had been witness to much of it. They had found Sheriff Brisbane, and were told that Brisbane would be riding into the area within the next two weeks. He had no real authority here, but he did have a posse at his disposal.

Jack knew that once the sheriff found out what Flint had orchestrated; he and his whole establishment would be ripe for the picking. Land grabbing was illegal after all, even though there was no law in this area to enforce that fact.

The next day, it was time to move on, but Jack had agreed to ride with Jewel back to the school. He really didn't want to, but honor kept him at her side until the gates of the school loomed ahead.

The same Indian woman met them at the gate and her

keys jingled as she turned the lock. Jewel grabbed her bag off her saddle and stood lookin up at Jack's sweating face. He stared down at her with the look of a man who had almost loved her but they both knew it was killing that defined Jack Ballard—not loving.

Jack said, "Goodbye, Jewel."

She took his hand from his saddle horn and pressed it to her cheek. Then she dropped it, stepped back and said, "Goodbye."

Jack turned his horse around and started to trot away from the school. He felt feverish and half ill but looked forward to leaving this parched land and sorrowful people behind. Suddenly, a cool, moist wind ruffled the hair on the back of his neck.

He pulled his horse to a stop and turned on the saddle to study the eastern sky. Big black thunderheads loomed on the near horizon, and he could see sheets of rain falling like gray curtains to the ground. His horse nickered and flicked his ears forward with interest.

Jack turned around and looked at the school where Jewel Swain and the Indian caretaker stood staring at the fast approaching storm. As if she sensed his gaze, Jewel turned toward him. Then she shook her head and lifted her arms in frustration. Jack knew just what she was feeling, and understood the irony of it.

If only the Bolt's had waited a few more days before letting their hate and anger get the best of them, if only Flint hadn't let greed overcome his good sense, if only the gunslinger Bob Trey hadn't come calling, if only … but, what was done was done, and there was no changing it now.

Jewel turned away and lifted her face to the rain, the

Indian woman danced in primal joy, and Jack clicked his tongue and rode slowly into the vast, West Texas plains.

Look for The Tortured Trail: A Jack Ballard Novel

BY LINELL JEPPSEN

REVENGE AND RETRIBUTION

Tortured Trail is the second novel in the straight shooting, fast moving, action-adventure Jack Ballard series.

In book one – No Man's Land – Ballard helped save a widow and her daughter from a hostile land grab in West Texas. Now, needing some cash, Jack has joined a cattle drive in Bandera, Texas and will serve as security and "Nighthawker" on the Western Trail heading toward Dodge City, Kansas.

The trail, however, is beset with trouble. Storms, cattle thieves, and Indian attacks follow Jack and the Triple T cattle drive, and the further north they go the worse it gets…

The Tortured Trail is the brain-child of the great

screenwriter Jeb Rosebrook, and is an edge-of-your-seat thriller!

AVAILABLE NOW

Linell Jeppsen

Linell Jeppsen is a writer of science fiction and fantasy. Her vampire novel, *Detour to Dusk*, has received over 44-four and five star reviews. Her novel *Story Time*, with over 130 4-and 5-star reviews, is a science fiction post-apocalyptic novel, and has been touted by the Paranormal Romance Guild, Sandy's Blog Spot, Coffee time Romance, Bitten by Books and 64 top reviewers as a five-star read, filled with terror, love, loss, and the indomitable beauty and strength of the human spirit. *Story Time* was also nominated as the best new read of 2011 by the PRG. Her dark fantasy novel, *Onio* (a story about a half-human Sasquatch who falls in love with a human girl), was released in December 2012 and won 3rd place as the best fantasy romance of 2012 by the PRG reviewers guild. Her novel, *The War of Odds*, won the IBD award for fantasy fiction and boasts 18 5-star reviews since its release in February of 2013. It also placed 2nd, as the best YA paranormal book of 2013 by the PRG.

Find more great titles by Linell Jeppsen here: http://wolfpackpublishing.com/linell-jeppsen/

Jeb Rosebrook

Journalist and novelist, **Jeb Rosebrook** was best known for his writing credits in film and television including the Sam Peckinpah film "Junior Bonner" starring Steve McQueen and Disney's "The Black Hole". He was nominated for two Writers' Guild of America television writing awards and an Emmy as co-writer of "I Will Fight No More Forever", the story of Chief Joseph. Film credits include the Sam Peckinpah directed classic, *Junior Bonner*, starring Steve McQueen and Disney's iconic sci-fi classic *The Black Hole*. Television credits for writing and co-writing and producing include numerous television films and mini-series, including Kenny Roger's *The Gambler*, *The Yellow Rose* and *The Outsiders*.

Jeb lived with his wife Dorothy in Scottsdale, Arizona until he passed away in August 2018.

Printed in Dunstable, United Kingdom

64365382R10118